LAVABULL

/ / / /

Piers Anthony
J.R. Rain

OTHER BOOKS BY J.R. RAIN
and PIERS ANTHONY

Aladdin Relighted
Aladdin Sins Bad
Aladdin and the Flying Dutchman
Dragon Assassin
Dolfin Tayle
Jack and the Giants
Lavabull
The Worm Returns

Published by
Crop Circle Books
212 Third Crater, Moon

Printed in the United States of America.

ISBN: 9781519004437

Chapter 1:
Lavender

Lavender looked at herself in the mirror. She saw a solid girl of 18, with an ample figure and hair so thick it was like a mat. Her eyes were like burning pits, her teeth like faceted stones, her hips like shapely anvils. So why were boys afraid of her?

Oh, she knew, really. She was hot, literally, especially in her core, and any young man who tried anything funny got burned in a very tender part. When she was a child the boys had tried to beat her up, and she had picked one up and hurled him into the sea. She read the minds of the others and prevented them from playing any nasty tricks on her. After that they had been more cautious, but when years later she grew breasts and hips, matching those of the other girls, they still had not wanted to date her despite her interest in socializing. It was frustrating. She was simply too much girl for the average boy. They preferred the soft, meek, shy, fragile efforts of the human girls.

Lavender was something else.

She paused, remembering the story of her parents. Her father was Jarvis, of human stock, who at age 28 had visited the volcanic island and encountered her ageless mother Lava. Lava was made of molten rock from the local volcano. She could read minds and shape herself into any form she chose. She was lonely and craved companionship and appreciation. So she catered to Jarvis, forming into a nymphly shape, fulfilling his dreams, and he promptly fell in love with her. Men were manageable, when a woman put her mind to it. Now they had been married 19 years and remained happy with each other, maybe in part because Lava remained as lovely as ever and constantly obliged his wishes before he even formed them. She didn't have to be burning hot, just hot enough to function comfortably for him.

That left Lavender, who was bored. She had no trouble with school, because anything she needed to know she read in the minds of the teachers and parroted back to them. She knew she wasn't actually very smart in the human fashion, but she didn't need to be as long as there was a smart human near. She could have fit in perfectly. She could have rendered herself all soft and cuddly and porous for a boy to handle, and cooled her core enough. So why hadn't she? This was where she differed from her mother. Lava was entirely shaped by Jarvis's desires, completely malleable. But Lavender was half human, and she had some human orneriness and ambition. She wanted to be someone in her own right, not just a sop for male interests.

She could have faked it, and gotten along fine. But she was at least the equal of any of the local boys, and wanted them to know it. Unfortunately the process of making them recognize it had also eliminated her as an object of romantic interest. She didn't have to guess at this; she read it in their minds. If she had wanted to become an endlessly obliging housewife like her mother, she had blown it. She wasn't really sorry.

And there it was. She was not like Lava. She had too much human orneriness in her. She wanted adventure, recognition, and romance, in that order. With a man who had similar ambitions. Yes, of course his first priority would be sex; that was simply the nature of the beast. She could handle that aspect. But then he should have the desire for adventure and recognition. He also needed to be powerful physically and forceful emotionally, with maybe a volcanic temper. Her grandfather was a volcano; she liked the type. And she wanted him to worship her much the way her father worshiped her mother, without being any less of a man. Was that such a tall order? It seemed it was, here on the island.

She turned away from the mirror and put on some clothes. She picked up a magazine her mother had been looking at. And saw him pictured there. The ideal man.

She promptly read the article. It seemed that this human man named Carl Gray had been a rodeo clown, distracting the bulls when they threw off their would-be riders. Then he had gotten caught by a bull, El Diablo, as a storm approached, and lightning had struck and fused them together. Now he was called The Bull. He had horns and a tail, was big and powerful, and it was said, ornery as hell. But his love life wasn't much. It seemed the women preferred to have pieces of tail apply to them, not to their boyfriends.

She knew it instantly: that was her man. But there was a problem: he lived in Rustic City, Arizona, while she lived on a Pacific volcano island. He didn't know she existed. So she would have to go to him.

She went to the kitchen where Lava was making a meal for Jarvis. "Mom—"

"Of course, dear," Lava said, knowing exactly what was on her mind. "I will persuade your father." Because he could not read minds and would be slow to understand.

"You want to go to the faraway mainland?" Jarvis exclaimed. "No way!"

"Dear," Lava murmured.

"But she has no connections there, no experience!"

Lava kissed him, then took him into the bedroom while Lavender took over the pot stirring. In fifteen minutes they emerged, and Jarvis gave his blessing. Lava's soft as putty persuasion invariably made him soft as putty too.

Armed with a change of clothing and a credit card, Lavender caught the next tourist ship and sailed for the mainland. She faked eating, taking very small portions as if dieting. She could eat and drink the human food, but did not need to, and there was no nutritive value in it for her. Not to mention the messy inconvenience of ejecting it from her body later. She did not advertise her nature, which meant that the men aboard saw her as a young pretty woman and promptly got the usual idea. When one corralled her in an isolated nook and angled for a kiss she did what she had to do. "I'm so sorry, but I have a bad skin malady where it doesn't normally show." She lifted her skirt to show a burning red rash on her bottom. She then superheated her lips and gave him a searing kiss he would not soon forget. He dashed off, yelping.

It wasn't that she couldn't have accommodated him. His mind showed her exactly what he wanted her to do, and she had made her core cool enough for this journey, as she didn't want to set fire to the bedsheets. It was that now that she had seen The Bull, she wanted to save her virginity for him alone. She let the rash fade out; it had served its purpose.

In due course the ship reached the port, and she caught a plane for Arizona. It was routine, until she picked up a mental distress signal. The pilot was going into a blackout. He didn't know it, but she did. She hurried forward, passing the plane's bathroom, where the copilot was having a siege of indigestion. She couldn't send her thought to warn him, but could read his knowledge of the plane. She kept that line open as she used the pilot's code to open the door, forged inside, and put her hands on the pilot as he lost consciousness. She lifted him out of his seat and set him on the floor beside it. Then she got in herself and used her mental line to the copilot to ascertain what to do. She put the craft on autopilot before it could go wrong.

The copilot returned. "What's this?" he demanded.

"He blacked out. I put it on auto," she said, rising from the seat.

"But you're no pilot!"

"True. But you are." She left the cockpit and returned to her seat in the body of the plane. No one had noticed her excursion except the stewardess, who had thought she might be in another kind of business with the pilots and kept her mouth shut.

When the plane landed without further event, she knew the copilot wanted to talk to her, so she waited until the craft emptied. "Who are you?" he demanded.

"Just a passenger."

"You may have saved all our lives."

"Please, I do not want notoriety."

"Neither do we," he said. "That was one close call. No one knew what was going to happen to him, least of all himself. We are getting him to the hospital now. You did exactly what was needed. The management will want to reward you."

"Please, no."

"But we owe you!"

"Please."

He gazed at her. "If word got out about this, there could be repercussions. Safety is our prime concern."

"I will say nothing."

He shook his head. "Silence suits us all. But if there is ever anything I can do in return, well, here's my card." He gave it to her.

"Thank you." She tucked it into a pocket and

left the plane. She doubted she would ever call him, but who knew for sure?

She took a taxi to the address of Carl Gray. Then she went to the door. She could tell by his mind that he was inside.

She paused to focus on her body. She could not change her shape instantly the way her mother could, because she was only half lava, but she could do it slowly. She sprouted a petite set of horns and a tail that showed under her skirt. She enhanced her bosom and broadened the spread of her hips. She dulled the fire in her pupils, as there was no need to reveal her inner fire. She was ready. She knew that The Bull's first impression of her would count for a lot. She wanted him to know instantly that she was his kind of woman. The details could come later.

When the door opened, she stood as a solid cowgirl, literally. She smiled.

Chapter 2:
The Bull

I was almost drunk.

Almost drunk wasn't going to do it, not when you've had the day I had. No, I needed to be all-the-way-drunk and forget this day ever happened. Which is why I fished out another beer from the case propped open on the floor next to me. A stack of similar cases sat in the far corner of the room. I had them shipped here weekly, brought in by two burly guys, who stacked them in piles of two, nearly up to the ceiling. Guys who stared at me the entire time. Guys who almost never made small talk with me. And if they did, it was often one-word answers. When they were done unloading, they got the hell out of here. I was even willing to bet they demanded hazard pay, too.

Not that I would hurt any of them. At least, not intentionally. This year alone, I had accidentally gored two people at a local feed store. Yeah, that's right. I buy my food at a feed store. You got a problem with that?

Luckily, beer goes down just fine. Maybe it's all that barley in it.

Despite my best intentions—and despite the copious booze already consumed—I found myself reviewing the day's events anyway. The day had started like any other: I had awoken in my living room, hung over and nearly buried in empty cans of beer. On this morning, my right horn had caught in my couch's arm, and I had spent a half minute trying to work it lose—that is, until my short temper had kicked in and I had ripped it free, veritably flinging the couch halfway across the room in the process.

In case you haven't guessed by now, yeah, I'm half bull and half man. The half-bull part is pretty obvious: I have a wide set of horns and whip-thin tail that, amazingly, I can control as surely as if it were any arm or a leg, a tail that sometimes seems to have a mind of its own.

This morning, as I stood among my dozens and dozens of empty beer cans, with my couch leaning against the far wall, I was vaguely aware of my tail absently reaching for nearby cans and tossing them into the empty beer case. My intention had been to clean the mess... and so my tail had begun the chore of doing so, even when my mind was, in fact, on my nearby cell phone. It had been my phone that had awakened me from my deep slumber. It had, I was certain, rang numerous times. Perhaps even dozens.

Grumbling, I crunched over empty cans to the low bookcase where my cell had been charging. I had long ago removed anything in my apartment that could break...or get caught in my horns. Nothing was on the walls, and no furniture was higher than my waist. I'd learned that lesson after going through three TVs in a month. Literally through. In fact, my entire apartment is crisscrossed with gouges and punctured with holes. Truth was, I had no business living in a small apartment. Not with this huge set of horns. Unfortunately, a bat cave didn't come with my condition, or a Fortress of Solitude. Sure, I might be one of the world's most recent superheroes, but I was presently living off my savings—savings that were drying up fast. I might be supernaturally strong and people had no problem calling on me for help, but they sure as hell didn't pay me for my time or help.

Which brings me to this morning. As I snatched up my phone, looking down at it in such a way that my left horn gouged a deep furrow along the top of the bookcase, I saw that I had missed, exactly, nineteen phone calls. Sighing, and using fingers that had, mercifully, remained human—I fumbled through the phone until I found the voice mail feature, and played back the messages. They were from, it turned out, the same woman. Requesting my help, over and over. Each message sounded more desperate than the last. Story of my life.

I clicked off the phone and set it down, rubbed my face. I looked like hell, I knew. Truth was, I looked like the world's biggest freak, with these horns and tail and hooves for feet. That lightning strike a few years ago had done a number on me. Not only had it seemingly fused me with the bull I had been wrangling, it had given me supernatural strength. Not just the strength of the bull, but ungodly strength, too. Or, perhaps, god-like strength. The horns might as well have been made from the hardest stuff in the known universe. The tips were so sharp as to cut through, literally, anything. Cut through, puncture through, tear through. I had done it all. My tail could often extend as far as I reasonably needed it to, easily four or five times its actual length. It served as a wonderful whip. And then there was my upper body strength, which was matched by only a few on this planet— and all were either superheroes or supervillains. Of course, my strength was enhanced even more when I actually charged—that is, when my back hooves kicked up a cloud of dust and undeniable rage filled me. Jesus, when that happened, I don't think anything on this planet could stop me. No wall. No fortified fortress. Maybe not even the big green guy, the Hulk. Certainly not any creep who threatens innocent people.

Which had been the basis of the panic calls this morning, the last of which had been just a few minutes ago. Some asshole was threatening his girlfriend. Threatening to kill her if she ever left him. And he was on the way to her house now. I had to replay one of the messages to remember the address—unfortunately, I wasn't given a super memory in the lightning strike—and then I was off. I charged down the center of the street, dodging cars, running faster and faster the angrier I got. And I was getting damn angry thinking about this asshole punk hurting this innocent girl. At least, she sounded innocent.

I rarely drive these days, although I have been saving up for a convertible, for obvious reasons. No, when I'm getting around my small town, I don't need to drive. I can run as fast or faster than most cars, especially in a lazy town like Rustic City. In no time at all I was at her small house on the edge of town. I slowed and assessed the situation.

The place was quiet. A truck was parked haphazardly in the driveway. Its driver's side door was open. So was the front door, from which issued a blood-curdling scream—and I was charging again.

This time through the front door, my wide shoulders shattering the door frame, and my even wider horns leaving two long grooves to either side of the door.

Snorting and my tail snapping this way and that, I found myself in an empty room. No, not entirely empty. I saw the cameras. Everywhere. High up in the ceiling. On tripods down hallways. On the kitchen table.

I had only recently learned that videos of me often go viral. As I break up a street gang or stop an armed bank robber or save a family from a fiery building—right, my thick bull hide is nearly impenetrable—video of my heroism spreads like a different kind of fire—wildfire. Apparently, I'm somewhat of a sensation on YouTube. All superheroes are.

As it turned out, I had been set up that morning by some college punks hoping to upload the next video to go viral. There had been no one in danger. No murderous ex-boyfriend. And so I gave them an eyeful. In a few minutes flat, the home was leveled and their cameras were destroyed, although one or two survived, somehow.

After all, that's the video I'm watching now on my laptop—myself destroying the home in a fit of rage—when there comes a knock on my front door. Now who the hell could that be?

Chapter 3:
Deal

There he stood, a giant bull of a man, literally. Wide-set horns, thin whip-like tail, the rest human, clad in last week's tattered cowboy suit. His body reeked of beer, and his mind reeked of frustration, futility, and shame.

Lavender had mentally prepared an introductory speech somewhere along the lines of, "Hello, Mister Bull. I am Lavender; I have admired you from afar, and I have come to be your loyal companion. Please take me in and let me show you what I can do for you. I do have useful talents, such as telepathy and the ability to change my shape." When he balked at such a sudden commitment, she would try to sweetly reason with him, leaning forward to give him a conducive peek of her ample bosom, to persuade him that she really did belong in his life. She did know how to make an impression on a man.

Instead her words preceded her thoughts.

"You're drunk!"

"Not yet, but trying hard," he said. "Whatever you're selling, I can't afford it and don't want it. Now get out of here before I vomit on you."

His mind was indeed in a vomitus state. She closed it off for the moment, as getting into it made her feel dizzy and disgusted. She should be able to handle this much on her own. It was clear he needed serious help.

"Aren't you going to invite me in?" Now she did the leaning forward bit.

"I told you I don't want any." But it required no mind reading to know that he did want something, and not just a peek at her bosom. He just didn't know how to express it.

"Thank you," she said. She pushed by him and entered the house. It was a total mess. "First let's make some space." The couch was upside down in the corner, half buried in beer cans. She gripped the edge of it and exerted her strength, turning it over. Then she looked up.

The Bull was staring at her. "You heaved it over!"

"Somebody needed to," she snapped. "Now clean up those cans so we have space for our feet. We have to talk."

"But you're a girl!"

"And now you're two for two. Are you going to get with the program?"

He seemed dazed. "Program?"

"Clean up the cans. Then sit down here with me so we can talk about our relationship."

He began to swell up belligerently. "Who the

hell are you to come in here and boss me around?"

This required a stronger measure. She stepped into him, used a hand to haul his head down, and kissed him soundly on the mouth.

It was as if a bomb went off in his skull. He had dreamed of something like this, which was one reason she did it. He secretly *wanted* to be governed by a woman, a pretty one, who understood and accepted him, as no other woman did.

Then he turned around and started using his tail to sweep the cans into piles in the corners. The main floor was soon bare.

Lavender sat on the couch and looked around. The room was in a sorry state, with horn-gores in the walls and crates of beer cans stacked in a far corner. He really was trying to drink himself into oblivion. Well, she would put a stop to that. When he had the empty cans clear, she caught his eye and patted the seat beside her.

Meekly, he obeyed, coming to sit where indicated. "You won't be needing that drug any more," she said. "We'll stack the crates in a back room and forget about them."

"But—"

"You drink to try to wash out your disgust with your own sorry state. That will change as of now. You have talents, but you're almost broke because people have been taking advantage of you. That has to stop."

"I know that!" he flared.

"Of course. I read it in your mind. You need to get organized."

"You read my mind?"

"I'm telepathic. You have a problem with that?"

He was beginning to focus. "I guess not. You're no ordinary girl."

"I'm not," she agreed. "Just as you're no ordinary man."

"You have horns. Tail."

"It's about time you noticed. I'm the same as you, at least in the ways that count. I'm only part human; the rest is a savage force of nature. You can't make it with an ordinary girl. They're afraid of you, and way too fragile." She got that too from his mind.

"Who the hell are you?"

"Rephrase that question, please."

"The hell I will! You can't just—"

He stopped, because she had kissed him again.

After the explosion in his skull dissipated, he regrouped. He was catching on that he was beaten in this respect. "I—I apologize for my language. What I mean is, why are you here?"

Now was the time for candor. "I'm a misfit, like you, as I said. I'm half human and half volcanic lava. Regular men are afraid of me, with good reason. I am literally too hot to handle, if I choose to be. I read about you, and decided that you could use my help and my love. You've got more power than brains, at least in the way you manage your life. I'm good at getting along, when I have to. I can help you manage, too." She knew from his mind that this was what he wanted.

"I do need help," he agreed. "But why should a pretty girl like you bother with me? Nobody else has."

"Because I think that together we can make a lot more of ourselves than we can apart. You're a lot more man than I've encountered elsewhere, so I've come to be your girlfriend. That's just the beginning."

"My girlfriend? The beginning? Are you insane?"

"Who knows, maybe? And this is the beginning of what I hope is a successful long-term collaboration. We aren't misfits to each other."

"Girlfriend," he said in wonder, picking up on that detail. "Do you even know what that means?"

"Yes. Remember, I know what's in your mind, including the passion. I can handle it, physically and emotionally. But you don't even know what romance is. You have no idea how to treat a girl you want to keep. So we won't get in bed together until you have a better notion. Now you need to take a bath to soak off some of that grime, and put on clean clothing."

"But—

"You need a girl who will love you. But for that you need to make yourself lovable. Or maybe more correctly love-a-bull. Or, better yet, lava-bull. I like it! Anyway, I'm telling you how."

"But—"

"Do I have to kiss you again?"

"You're serious?"

He was catching on to what she offered. He desperately wanted it. But she was not about to settle for drunk and disorderly. "I can strip you and scrub you and dress you if you wish. Your body hardly matters when I know your mind. So—"

She was interrupted by the ringing of his cell phone. She got up and fetched it. "This is the residence of The Bull," she said. "What can we do for you?"

"He's got a secretary?" the voice asked, amazed.

"More than that. Get to the point."

"Listen, my company needs a load of tanks of diesel fuel, and we need them now. The regular delivery was stopped by a wreck. A damn drunk driver hit it and knocked the wiring loose. We need a man to put a chain on that wreck and haul it to the factory, and the local towing service won't touch it this late in the day. It's only a mile. The Bull can do it."

"Yes he can," she said evenly. "What fee do you offer?"

"Fee? The Bull doesn't charge a fee."

"He does now."

"This is outrageous!"

"Then get someone else to haul your truck. Nobody's sponging off The Bull any more. Spread the word."

There was a pause. She wished she could read his mind, but that worked only at close range. So she was bluffing.

"Fifty dollars," the man said.

"Two hundred dollars."

"Seventy five."

"A hundred and fifty."

"A hundred."

"Deal," she agreed, hoping they weren't being

taken. "Where's the truck?"

In moments she had the location. "We'll be there."

She disconnected and turned to The Bull. "Postpone that bath. We've got a deal. Where's your car?"

"Still in the shop from the last time I wrecked it. But I can run to the site."

"I can't. I can do a lot, but I'm no distance runner."

"Then I'll carry you."

She nodded. "Good enough. Let's go."

They exited the house, he picked her up and slung her over his shoulder, and ran at an incredible speed. Any ordinary girl would have been wiped out by the rough bouncing, but of course she wasn't. Still, in due course she would teach him how to carry a lady. She didn't really like having her legs over his shoulder and her skirt being blown up by the wind so that any oaf could see her exposed bottom.

They reached the site. The Bull set her down. There was a chain on the truck. He took that and anchored it to the hoop in front. She got into the cab. He hauled, and the truck was moving at a good clip, considering.

At the factory the manager came out to thank them. "You're welcome," Lavender said and held out her hand for the money. He gave it to her and she tucked it away. "We're done here, Bull. Let's go home."

The not really odd thing was that the manager approved. He knew The Bull needed supervision and a woman with gumption and a really tough hide. Then he would no longer be almost as much a menace to the community as an asset. Of course he wouldn't say so openly, at least not to The Bull. But it was in his mind.

The Bull picked her up again, same as before. She knew the manager's eyes were bugging as her skirt flew up; she read his appreciative peek. Couldn't be helped, this time.

Back at his house she took over again. "Bath," she ordered. "New clothes."

This time he didn't try to argue. He went to the bathroom.

"And soak your face in cold water," she called after him. "You need to be sober for our next discussion."

Then she sat down and let go in a wash of reaction. She had played it tough because it was an emergency, but now she would have to persuade a sober and halfway sensible man that he really did want her in his life. That might not be easy.

Chapter 4:
Villainous

World Media Transmission #1

Greetings, I am Villainous.

If you are hearing these words for the first time, it means one of two things: you are about to die, or I have failed.

I do not plan to fail. I have taken careful steps not to fail. In fact, I have devoted my entire life to carrying out this plan, to assure its success—and to assure the total destruction of the earth.

You see, I have grand plans. In fact, no one has ever accused me of not being ambitious. Sure, they've accused me of everything else under the sun —many nasty, nefarious, villainous things (and most of them are true, let me assure you)—but never have I been accused of thinking small.

And this is big. Very, very big.

Perhaps the biggest ever.

Nothing short of the total destruction of this wretched rock we call planet Earth.

You see, I think we have mostly gotten it all wrong. I think we could have done a better job of managing this planet, of managing its people, and managing its resources. I think we are rapidly heading to destruction, and I just can't have that. Not on my watch, and not when I can do something about it.

I do not want money. I do not want new technologies. I want only the chance to hit the reset button. I have plans for this planet. Big plans. New ideas. New governments. New family units. New everything. We are few, but we are ambitious, to say the least.

But I can't implement these plans if the rest of the world is hell bent on destroying itself and its precious resources. And I certainly don't intend to be a target for the world's mightiest powers.

And so, I have disappeared from the limelight, so to speak. You might even recognize my voice. If so, you are correct. However, I go by a new name now. It's only a temporary name, you see. It fits my mood. It fits my current temperament. After all, why should names be so permanent? Who made that rule up?

New ideas, new names, new everything.

I am Villainous, and if you are hearing my words, it might already be too late. After all, I have cooked up a helluva scheme. And soon all the world will tremble.

But for now, you might have a few minutes, or a few days. After all, even I can't predict when a volcano will explode, try as I might.

But let me assure you, there is no stopping the

damage... and the resulting poison that will spread. Sure, some of you might survive in your bomb shelters, and some of you might even make it a few months or years. But know this: I have thought of everything, and every last one of you—every last human and primate, that is—will understand what death is. Your destruction is imminent.

So, I want to thank you for participating in the human race.

Except now the race is finished.

Game over.

Chapter 5:
Decision

Lavender turned on the TV while waiting for The Bull to complete his cleanup. What came on at first confused her, then made her wonder. It seemed to be a repeating printed message from an anonymous source, threatening the destruction of the human species, and indeed, all primates. That was to say, monkeys who walked on two legs.

Oh—it was a cheap video adventure. She had seen those before. The end of the world was a favorite theme. It always got saved at the last moment.

Except that there were no commercials, and no breaks. When the printed message concluded, it immediately started over, without change. Also, normally the videos were acted out, not displayed like the pages of a book. Curious.

The Bull emerged from the bathroom. He was clean and dressed, looking almost handsome. He did not sway as he walked, indicating that he was well on the way to being sober. It was a vast improvement.

"Okay, now we can talk," he said. "But first, how about another kiss? Or are you just playing me the way everyone else does?"

He was definitely interested, and she liked that. But now, ironically, she was going to have to change the subject. "One kiss. Then you have to watch the TV."

"Who cares about the TV? It's all junk."

She went to him and kissed him. He liked that even better sober than when he was tipsy. "There will be more as we work things out," she said. "But first I need your judgment on this TV program. I'm new to the mainland and there are things I don't properly understand. Do you think it's a joke?" She took his hand and had him sit down beside her on the couch.

He looked. "Yes, must be a joke. Hackers trying to make me think I've got to save the world. Make a fool of me yet again."

"I'm not sure of that. It doesn't seem to be directed at you."

The phone rang. Lavender picked it up. "Yes?"

"Are you that new girl with The Bull?"

"Yes. Who are you and what do you want?"

"This is Ian, your neighbor to the north."

The man was just out of mind reading range. "Hello, neighbor."

"Have you seen the TV?"

"It's got an end of the world program."

"That's it. Think it's a joke?"

26

So he was concerned too. This seemed legitimate. "We were wondering. Want to talk with The Bull?"

"Yes, please."

She handed the phone to The Bull. "Neighbor to the north named Ian. He's watching the same program."

"I know him. He's legit." He lifted the phone. "Hi, Ian. You're getting it too?" He paused, listening. Lavender could have picked up the other voice through The Bull's mind, but didn't bother; this was minor interaction, incidentally establishing her place in The Bull's life.

"And the other neighbors? Overriding their normal programs? I agree: this is weird." He disconnected.

Weird indeed. "Let's walk around the block," Lavender said.

"Why?"

"So I can read minds as we pass other people. I need to get reasonably close, like within about talking distance. Then we'll know how widespread this is."

He looked at her, his thoughts percolating. He didn't quite believe in her permanence, and feared she would disappear without ever being more than an in-name-only girlfriend. Another tease.

"It's not like that," she snapped. "What use is a girlfriend to you, if the world ends tomorrow?"

He sighed. "We'll walk around the block."

They walked. She reached out with her mind, catching the occupants of the houses they passed, at the fringe of her range. They were watching the broadcast with amazement, annoyance, and dawning fear. It was happening to everyone.

They returned to the house. "So it's not just a joke on me," The Bull said.

"Not," she agreed. "But what *is* it?"

"Smells to me like a brag. Someone who hates us just had to crow a little about his evil plot."

Then the message disappeared. It was replaced by a regular TV announcer. "Folks, we regret the interruption of our normal programming," he said. "Hackers got into the system and had their illicit fun. Ignore the 'Villainous' message. It was simply an ugly practical joke. It appears to have been put on worldwide at the same time. It is rapidly being eradicated."

"That's a relief," The Bull said. "At least this time the joke's on someone else."

"This time," she agreed. Then she remembered something. "Oh—here's your money."

"Money?"

"The fee you earned for hauling that truck. A hundred dollars in cash." She dug it out of her purse and handed it to him.

"Oh, yeah." He really hadn't tuned in on the money.

"Now about our relationship—" She broke off, reading his mind. "All right, we'll talk this way." She got up, moved over, and sat on his lap. "Girlfriend style."

"Yeah," he said, pleased, putting his arms around her.

"Don't worry, I won't break or freak out. You know I'm half lava, hot inside. I can cool down where it counts when I put my mind to it, but you don't want to rush it. My form is mostly my conscious shaping, including the horns and tail. When I sleep, I may settle into a lump of hot rock. Can you handle that?"

"Yeah," he said, drawing her in close. "Same's you handle my being half bull."

"That's why I came here. I figured you'd understand about how I'm different."

"Yeah." He absolutely loved having a real live girl in his arms. One who could handle him.

"I think I should handle your finances, because —" She stopped, because he agreed. He gave her back the money.

She laughed. "How can we have a comprehensive dialog if you agree before I finish my thought?"

"What I want doesn't require much talking."

"Don't I know it! You see me as a heifer in heat. I'm hot all right, but not quite that way. However—"

The phone rang again. She took it, again. "The Bull's residence. His assistant speaking."

"Girlfriend," he said loud enough for the phone to pick it up.

"I am calling from the limousine parked outside your house," the voice said. "Please join me immediately."

"Now wait a minute," Lavender protested. "We don't find these jokes funny."

"Read my mind."

He knew about that? She reached out and caught the mind in the limo. It was at the edge of her range, but that was enough. "Oh, my."

"Say nothing," the voice said. "Just join me. Both of you." The connection quit.

"Huh?" The Bull asked.

"That was a representative of the Secretary of Defense," she murmured in his ear. "We need to meet with him in the limo, which is secure from electronic surveillance. It is not a joke."

"What has any such person to do with me?"

She put her finger against his lips. "I think we're in deeper than we know."

They went out to the waiting limo. The door opened and they got in, joining a seated man.

"Read my mind," he repeated.

She did. Up close she had a much better take on him. He was absolutely legitimate. But it was so complicated that she backed off. "Maybe you'd better spell it out aloud," she said. "The Bull is not a mind reader."

"Of course," he said as the chauffeured limo moved out. "The recent broadcast, as nearly as we can ascertain, was not a joke. True, it was put on by hired hackers, but they are losing their appetite for it as they come to realize that they, too, are included in the destruction. We are up against a homicidal madman. I use that term advisedly, as we are not at all sure he is human."

"We're not exactly human either," Lavender said sharply.

"Exactly. That's why we need you. Villainous seems to be the representative of a group of, for want of a better term, crossbreeds, though they are not exactly that. We call them animen, though they are female too. One of you is a merger of human and lava, the only cross with the inanimate we know of. The other is a merger of human and bull. This sort of thing has been happening rarely, but all over the world. There are crosses with orcas—that is, killer whales—elephants, giant squid, bears, and perhaps others we don't yet know of. They all have human intelligence and animal strengths. You, Lavender, are the only telepathic one we know of; perhaps that is a quality of the volcano that sired your mother. The one who calls himself Villainous seems to be a human-polar bear merger. The polar bears are in desperate straits as human-caused global warming melts their icy habitat and human settlements encroach on their arctic domain and human over-fishing depletes their food supply. He hates mankind and means to exterminate it."

He paused for a breath, then continued. "It seems they have devised a kind of gaseous poison that affects only primates, killing them within hours. Human beings are primates. Their problem has been distribution. Now, if the broadcast is to be believed, they have found a way: insert it in the lava chamber of a volcano, and let a subsequent eruption disburse it into the atmosphere. Global air currents would spread it across the globe soon enough, bringing human death wherever it goes."

"Wow," The Bull said. "Why tell us?"

"Because you represent a unique combination of talents that we desperately need for this mission: strength and telepathy, with a volcanic connection. We need you to locate the key volcano and remove the poison before it erupts. Once it erupts it will be too late. Humanity may be doomed."

"You mean, unless they're bluffing," Lavender said.

"We can't afford to take the risk that they're bluffing."

"You don't know which volcano?" The Bull asked.

"That's right. We don't know. We will provide you with all necessary transport to any and all volcanoes, and all assistance you require. You will be top secret agents, as of now." He smiled briefly. "If you are concerned about money, we will pay you ten thousand dollars a day, or more if you demand it. The service we require is of course priceless."

"Well," The Bull started.

"We need to consider," Lavender said.

"Of course. Will an hour do?"

"It should."

The limo drew to a stop right before The Bull's residence. They got out and walked to the house. "What's this about considering?" he asked inside. "Of course we want to help save the world, and the money's good."

"Big decisions of any nature should always be considered carefully," she said. "Here's the thing: we are what they call animen. We'll probably be immune to that poison. We'll surely be welcomed into the new order, if it comes."

"So?"

"Which side are we on?"

Chapter 6:
Animen

We had an hour. I only needed seconds, but I could see that Lavender was having a tougher time with it.

"Isn't your father human?" I asked.

"He is, but perhaps we can convince Villainous to spare him."

"And you would want to negotiate with a man —or animan—who is willing to kill billions of people?"

She shook her head, and I saw literal steam waft up from under her collar. "No, of course not. I'm sorry, I don't know what I was—"

I took her perfectly formed face and cradled it in a hand that could, if called upon, crush skulls or snap trees. And her face was "formed" too. I had no doubt that Lavender could take on any shape she wanted. That she had picked such an appealing form was a form of manipulation of course. I wondered what her natural form looked like. Or was I seeing it?

Didn't matter, not with a creature who could take on any shape she wanted—and the shape she had chosen was a damn fine one indeed.

"Thank you, big guy, now where is all of this leading?" she said, following my train of thoughts.

"It's understandable that you would want to be like others of your own kind—hell, picturing myself with other half-breeds, and being accepted—is damn appealing. But being accepted is one thing. Killing billions is another. I can live as an outcast. But I couldn't live with myself knowing I didn't try to stop this madman."

"Point taken. I really am a good person. I just had..."

"A momentary lapse?"

"I was going to say a rough life. I was mostly alone. Kids avoided me, especially after I threw one of them into the sea."

I laughed at the image, then grew somber as I remembered the very real threat we were all facing, human and non-human. After all, what kind of world would remain, if run by this madman?

"Good point," said Lavender, picking up my thoughts like a champ. "So what's the plan?"

Admittedly, I liked seeing her human side. It was a pleasant change from her smoldering lava side, which she'd been laying on kinda thick since her arrival. I also liked seeing her uncertainty, too. As tough as she came across, she was no superhero. Not yet, anyway. I liked being needed, and I also liked taking charge, too. I'd only been in the superhero business for a short time, but I had more experience at it than she did.

"First, let's tell the representative we're in."

We did so, and were told that a military transport plane was waiting at the nearby Davis-Monthan Air Force Base, along with a crack team of Navy SEALS who would be assisting us. Apparently, another team of superheroes—a more famous team whose exploits were often featured on the big screen, were given the task to find Villainous himself. Two teams: one searching for the rigged volcano (us), and another searching for the bastard himself. Seemed about as effective a plan as we could have, under the circumstances. Of course, Villainous had had years to concoct his own plan, and to put safeguards in place. I suspected finding him and his lair would be a challenge, even for an experienced team of superheroes.

"Never mind that," said Lavender, reading my mind, as usual. "We have a volcano to find." She shot a glance at the representative. "Speaking of which, how did you know I was here? More important, how did you know about my family's volcanic roots? And, quite frankly, how did you get here so fast? The message was only recently aired —" She paused, reading his mind. "The apartment is bugged. You've been listening to us."

My mouth dropped and I felt the heat rising in my face. I am quick to anger, as bulls are wont to be. And when I get angry, I tend to want to destroy things. Take that last house for instance.

The representative's smarmy smile faltered when he saw me puff out. No doubt my face was taking on a shade of red, too, which tends to happen. More than anything, I see red. Blinding red that fills me with rage and hate.

"Easy, Bull," he said. "We try to keep tabs on all superheroes. At least, all *new* superheroes. We have to know whose side they are on. We have to know if they pose a threat and need to be neutralized. You have proven, time and again, to be on the side of good. And, yes, Lavender, we were aware of your arrival this morning. We've been frantically looking into your background ever since, and were shocked, to say the least, by your ancestry. There's not a lot of people on earth who can say their grandfather is a volcano."

"That doesn't explain how you got here so fast."

"I'm based out of Davis-Monthan. We received advanced word that something big was about to get announced. That the world media had, in fact, been hijacked. We were all put on alert. Lavender's arrival can only be described as serendipitous."

"Seems legit to me," I said.

Lavender scanned his thoughts some more, frowned, then said, "You're hiding something else, Mr. Brookstone."

The representative smiled, and some of his oiliness returned. "We have been well-versed in compartmentalizing our secrets from mind readers, Ms. Lavender. You are not the only telepath on earth. And we have many, many secrets."

"Cut the crap," I said to him, sitting up. "The way I see it, we need to find this rigged volcano, and fast." I looked at Lavender. "Any ideas?"

She bit her lip in a way that I found adorable. Finally, she nodded. "I do. Take us to the nearest volcano. Active or dormant, it doesn't matter."

Mr. Brookstone blinked, then pulled out his phone, swiped it on, used his thumbs to rapidly do a Google search, and reported: "The closest is Sunset Crater Volcano, just north of Flagstaff, about one hundred miles away."

"Then that's where we need to go."

"I'll let the pilot know."

"What's the plan?" I asked.

She rested her hand on my thigh. "We're about to awaken a dormant volcano."

"Is that safe?"

"For me, yes. But the volcano might be annoyed."

"You speak as if it's a person."

"It's a kind of person. It's an entity all its own, and it might have answers for us."

Chapter 7:
Volcano

The plane oriented on a private strip near
Flagstaff, and Lavender admired the Painted Desert
nearby before they landed. She liked landscapes,
being half rock herself. An inconspicuous mini bus
took them north to the Sunset Crater Volcano. "This
should be interesting," Brookstone remarked.

Lavender didn't respond to his borderline
sarcasm. She knew what she was doing. What she
didn't know was how the volcano would react to
being roused from its slumber. She was in a position
to know that volcanoes could be irritable; if one got
angry, it was best to be far away. She would have to
tread carefully, physically and mentally. But this
was the only way she could see to make progress on
their mission.

They pulled up at the fringe of the volcano.
Lavender saw immediately that it was only a
shadow of its former greatness. Its contours had

weathered down and brush had overgrown much of it. That brush would not have dared encroach, in the volcano's heyday.

"What now?" The Bull asked.

"I need to commune with the mountain. It's asleep now. It may not like being waked. The rest of you should probably withdraw a space."

"How far is a 'space'?" Brookstone asked snidely.

"Three miles should suffice."

He laughed. "How about three hundred feet?"

That was ludicrous, but she was annoyed. "Suit yourself."

The bus backed off about a tenth of a mile, leaving the two of them. "Maybe you should join them," she told The Bull.

"I'm with you. A little shaking won't hurt me. Besides, I'm curious what you're up to."

She liked him, but he too maybe could use a lesson. "As you wish."

Now she doffed her clothes and sat on the ground, increasing her contact with it. She let her posterior melt somewhat, melding with the soil beneath, which had formed from an ancient lava flow. There was an affinity.

"Wow," The Bull said appreciatively. "You've got some ass. I mean that in the most admiring way."

"I know it. Now please be silent while I commune."

He shut his mouth, but his eyes remained on her bare body, and his thoughts were rampant.

"Your mind too," she snapped. "This isn't your

bedroom."

He tried to stifle his thoughts, managing to mute them somewhat. That helped.

Lavender reached out with her mind, the way she did when communing with her grandfather. She searched down through the layers of igneous rock, seeking the heat below. There would be a magma chamber, sealed over, quiescent, but still the mind and heart of the volcano.

She found it. *Mountain mind*, she thought. *Hearken to me!*

There was a stir of awareness. *Who are you?*

I am Lavender, half human granddaughter of an island volcano. But Grandfather is far away, so I must commune with you instead. I apologize for waking you, but my need is dire.

The awareness expanded. A powerful mind force coalesced around her. *There is lava in you.*

Yes. I am imperfect, a crossbreed, but I stem from volcanic lineage.

What volcano?

She presented the mental signature of her grandfather.

I know of him. All volcanoes connect via the subterranean labyrinth.

Yes. Grandfather told me that if I were ever in desperate need, far away from him, to come to whatever volcano I could reach and he would help me. So I have come to you.

The mind intensified. *What need is this?*

She could have told him about the threat to human existence. But she knew that volcanoes hardly cared about human concerns; men were mere flies on the hide of elephants. Instead she told him about the way the animen were using a volcano. How they were planting chemical bombs that the heat of the erupting volcano would disperse into the atmosphere. *The humans do not like this. They may nuclear bomb volcanoes to get rid of the chemical.* She sent an image of the kind of destruction such a bomb could do to an innocent volcano.

The volcano reacted. *The nerve! We do not want this!*

Of course not, she agreed. *But it is the plan of the animen. They are using you to destroy their enemy.*

The volcano pondered. The more he pondered, the hotter he got. His magma chamber swelled, pushing the rock above it upward. Bushes and trees were shaken.

"Yow!" That was The Bull, reacting to being jostled by a small earthquake. The government men were out of ready telepathic range, but she got a mental jolt as their bus was bounced and shaken. Well, she had warned them.

What do you want of me? the volcano asked.

I want to eliminate the poison vapor bomb, so that the humans will not fear volcanoes and seek to decimate them. It is in a volcano, but I do not know which one. It is my hope that you can commune with your brethren and learn which one has been been molested by the animen. Then I can go to remove the vapor bomb, and there will be peace between the volcanoes and mankind.

The volcano considered. His heat continued to grow, and the ground shoved upward and cracked open. Super-heated gas speared out from the new vents, incinerating the remaining vegetation. The Bull danced about, avoiding the steaming cracks; even he was not immune to this kind of heat. It did not bother Lavender, of course.

The government men had finally gotten the word. The bus was speeding away from the action, seeking the three-mile distance she had recommended. They were learning.

I am contacting the network, the volcano reported. *Querying for such intrusions.*

Thank you, she thought, relieved that he had decided to cooperate. It certainly could have been otherwise.

Well, there's a certain hot sweetness about you, lava child, he thought.

Lavender had practiced using human sex appeal on human men. Did it work also on volcanoes?

The ground she sat on lifted higher as the heat of the volcanic outreach increased. Lava welled up, filling the cracks, flowing down the new slopes. An acrid cloud of gas floated just above the level of her head. The Bull danced closer to her, ducking down, realizing that her perch was relatively stable.

Three volcanoes have been molested, the volcano reported.

Three! Where are they?

The volcano projected a spherical map of the globe. The spots were widely scattered around it. Lavender grabbed it with her mind, making it her own. *Thank you!* she repeated.

Now let me sleep in peace.

Welcome, Grandfather. It was an honorary term.

The swelling of the earth abated. The ground slowly sank, the crevices sealing up. The radiation of heat diminished. The cloud thinned. The volcano was returning to quiescence. It would be a while before things were normal, but there would be no eruption.

"Wow!" The Bull exclaimed. "That was some thrill ride!"

Lavender disengaged her lava from the ground and reshaped it into a human posterior. She stood. "Don't touch me yet," she warned. "I'm too hot."

"I'll say!"

They walked across the ruined landscape toward the bus. When she had cooled enough, Lavender put her clothing back on.

"Did you get what you sought?" he asked.

"Yes. There are three volcanoes we have to check."

"Three! What ones are they?"

"I do not know."

"But—" His mind was all confusion.

"I have a map."

"Oh."

In due course, they reached the bus, now parked in the safe area. Brookstone came out to meet them. "We were afraid we'd lost you!" he said.

"You forget my origin," Lavender said, stifling her urge to be smug.

"Any more volcanoes we have to visit?"

"Three." She loved the mental cringe she felt.

"Where?"

"I don't know."

"You don't know!"

"Now I need a globe of the world."

"We can show one onscreen."

"No. A real one."

"We'll do what we can." He no longer questioned her needs; his arrogance had been replaced by frustrated respect.

They drove to Flagstaff and found an old fashioned curio store. It had an old fashioned globe. Lavender focused on it, aligning the map in her head with the one of the globe.

She found one of the sites. "Pinotubo," she announced.

"Pinotubo!" Brookstone exclaimed, punching it into his genius phone internet connection for information. "That's the one that blew out so much ash it cooled the whole planet by a degree for several years!"

"That must be the one," she agreed.

She found another. "Thera. Or Santorini. Both names are on it."

"And that's the one that destroyed the empire of Crete over two thousand years ago. Those cones are dangerous."

She found the third. "Mount St. Helens."

"And that's the one in the state of Washington that wiped out a whole landscape."

"The gas bomb is in one of those," she said.

"One? Then why did they go to three?"

"I can tell you that," The Bull said. "They wanted to hide it so we couldn't just zero in on one and nullify it. By the time we check all three, spaced around the world, the real one may go off. And I'll bet that even the animen who placed them don't know which of the three is the real one, so Lavender can't read any minds and get it that way. And I'll bet further that they're not just sitting there. There will be animen guarding each one. Even your Navy Seals will have trouble handling bear or tiger or orca men."

"So might a bull man," Brookstone said, recovering his snideness.

"And suppose one's telepathic?" The Bull asked.

That set Lavender back. She had been the only telepath involved in their mission so far. What would she do if one of the enemy could read her mind as readily as she could read others?

This mission promised to be more of a challenge than she had first thought.

Chapter 8:
Battalions

"Stay here," said Brookstone, pulling out his phone. He stepped out of the curio shop and into the bright Arizona sunlight, where he proceeded to speak with what appeared to be some urgency. No surprise there. I watched him with some urgency, too, if that was possible.

"Where does he get off telling us to wait?" said Lavender, hands on her hips and steam literally coming out of her ears.

"He's the one who controls the planes out of here," I said. "Unless you can sprout lava wings, we're grounded until we figure out what to do next."

"Some superheroes we are, at the mercy of some bureaucratic ass."

"For now," I said.

"And, yes, I can sprout wings, for your information. But not for flying—for gliding. I used to do it as a kid. I would jump off my grandfather's highest point, and glide down for nearly an hour. Pure heaven."

"Okay, now that I gotta see!" I spun the globe idly. "So what's he saying out there?"

She shook her head. "His mind is shielded. I think he does it automatically, out of habit, and I don't read lips."

"And he's out of my hearing range," I said. Bulls may not be known for their hearing, but we can pick up high frequency sounds beyond normal human hearing. Trust me, it's not all it's cracked up to be. Try sleeping when you can hear your neighbor's snoring from across the street!

"Oh, boohoo," said Lavender, reading my thoughts. "Try explaining to your classmates that your grandpa is a volcano."

I spun the globe again, this time faster than I'd intended. It leaped off its axis, and shot down the aisle of the curio shop, knocking over a postcard display case and grazing the bum of the old lady who ran the shop. The globe finally came to a rest at the far end of the store, leaving a minor trail of destruction in its wake.

"Oops," I said.

"Like a bull in a china shop," said Lavender, laughing.

"If you two are done screwing around, it's time to go."

I fished out a couple of twenties from my workout sweats that I tended to favor these days. There wasn't a shirt on earth that would fit me, unless you wrapped a bed sheet around me. And there was no way in hell I was walking around in a bed sheet. I am who I am, and what I am is a beast of a man, in every sense of the word. I left the twenties on the counter.

When we were were settled in the mini-bus—and after my horns were guided carefully through the open windows on either side—Brookstone explained. "We have teams converging on all three locations as we speak—"

"But—" began Lavender.

"But nothing. You two are new to the hero game, and you have served your purpose, for now. You gave us intel that would have been impossible to get otherwise. Now, let's just sit back and let our teams take down the animen."

"And what about Villainous?" I asked.

"We have another team of heroes searching for him. A *proven* team of heroes. We can watch the action unfold from the base."

***

And so we did.

We took a seat in the Command and Control Room, or C&C, which was located deep in the base, and could have doubled as NASA's mission control. Banks of computers were everywhere, manned by what Brookstone called "spooks," or data intelligence gatherers. Massive screens surrounded us on either side. Most prominent were the three screens before us, which featured a very grim President of the United States. Other screens displayed the heads of other states. There was the

German Chancellor, the British Prime Minister, and Russia's President. There were others, too, all watching their own feeds, all waiting and seeing just what would happen.

"We have three teams on standby, waiting to hear from our remote viewer in Langley, Virginia."

"Remote viewer?" I asked.

"Distant seeing. It's a form of clairvoyance. Don't ask me how it works, but once our guy locks onto a target, he can scan it from a distance."

"What's he looking for?" I asked.

"Something that would indicate a viable threat. Possibly a thermonuclear warhead. Now sit here quietly and watch the fireworks," said Brookstone. "Oh, and don't touch anything."

The representative left to join a group of men at a long table near the front of the command room, leaving us alone. "I'm really beginning not to like that guy," I said.

"I didn't like him the moment I read his mind," said Lavender. "He's hiding something. I'm sure of it."

"Well, we might as well watch the show. There's nothing else on TV. Hey, do you think there's a vending machine around here? I'm starving."

***

I had barely come back with my bag of M&M's when we got the first round of bad news. As I took my seat next to Lavender, the entire C&C was in an excited uproar, including the heads of state who were consulting now with those closest to them.

"What did I miss?" I asked.

"They're not saying much, but I can pick up the general thoughts of the room. From what I gather, the distant viewer confirmed the package deposited inside Mount Pinatubo is a fake. The team there is going to engage the animen anyway."

She pointed to the screen to the far right, and what I saw was a barely discernible mess. The images were mostly from head-mounted cameras, and I caught brief glimpses of flashing gunfire—and teeth and claws. The animen there were putting up a furious fight. Until one after another, the head gear winked off. One such gear landed on its side, and I realized I was looking at a fallen soldier. A bear-beast appeared in frame, bounding over the rocky soil. It stopped at the fallen soldier, raised a mighty paw, and slashed down. The image turned black.

I looked away. Poor bastard.

"More US and British soldiers are pouring into Pinatubo," reported Lavender. "Meanwhile, the focus now is on Mount St. Helens in Washington State, where a joint US and Russian team is waiting on standby."

I marveled at my new girlfriend—and just saying that sounded strange and exciting—whose head jerked this way and that, as she continuously scanned the thoughts of those in the room. The action on Pinatubo continued, until I finally looked away. I might be a new superhero, but I didn't like watching men die... and so viciously, too.

"Mount St. Helens is a fake, too," reported

Lavender. "The teams there are engaging the animen, as well."

And so they did. I saw gunfire and explosions and twisted bodies and death everywhere. I looked away.

"The focus is now on Thera in Crete, where a battalion of European Union commandos is waiting."

We waited. Meanwhile, the action on the other screens continued, as good men died, fighting against creatures that were nothing short of monsters. Creatures like me. How long before I was viewed as such a monster? How long before the men in this room turned on me as well?

The group of top brass closest to the big screen leaped to their feet.

"Confirmed in Thera," reported Lavender nearly as fast. She sat forward. "A thermonuclear warhead is buried deep in the magma there. It's not quite on a timer. Instead, it appears set to go off once the outer shell of nickel has been melted away. According to the distant viewer, we are hours away from an explosion. The battalion is engaging."

And the animen were waiting, and they were many. They appeared on screen from seemingly everywhere, bounding over land and bursting from the sea. Great cats and gorillas and sharks. Creatures I couldn't quite recognize. As the slaughter continued, I wondered how the other animen had formed. I thought my situation had been a fluke, with the lightning strike. Perhaps the lightning had just been on the way. Or perhaps the lightning hadn't been such a fluke after all. I considered that maybe Villainous had created his own soldiers, and somehow I got caught up in it. Perhaps an errant lightning strike, all while he was creating his soldiers elsewhere. Something to ponder.

More explosions, more carnage, and from what I could tell on the big screen, the European soldiers were being decimated. At the least, they were making no progress, and time was slipping away.

"The distant viewer just confirmed that the volcano is lined with poison. Megatons of poison. All set to explode into the atmosphere as soon as the nuclear bomb goes off."

"This just keeps getting better and—"

"Shh! Hold on. They're talking about us, Bull. They're desperate. There's something here, on the base. Something highly experimental." Lavender looked at me. "It's a teleporter."

"A tele-what?"

"Teleporter... and they want to send us into the volcano."

Chapter 9:
Burning Lady

"Send us to Thera?" The Bull asked. "What can we do there that their crack troops can't? We may be animen, but we're just two to their dozens."

Lavender cobbled her answer together from what she was reading telepathically and her own thoughts. "You're an animan. You could mix with them and they'd think you're on their side. I am in a similar form, a cowgirl. In all the rush of battle, they wouldn't think to check our authenticities. I am also telepathic. I can read their minds to discover whether there is any way to turn off that bomb before its casing melts. Usually there's a way, in case the personnel are delayed getting out; I pick that up from the minds here. If we turn it off, the eruption will melt it instead of setting it off, and there will be no nuclear dispersal to impregnate the entire mountain with the poison. Their end-of-the-world bomb will fizzle."

He shook his horny head. "I may be bullheaded, but even I can see that this is risky as hell. There may be no way to turn it off, but if there is, there may be no animan there who knows it. If there is one who knows, they may recognize us as not in their group, if they have cohorts that know each other the way regular military units do. You can't read any minds if they attack us the moment they see us. Maybe we can be teleported in, but I'll bet we can't be teleported out again. We'll be on our own in hell."

These were apt thoughts. How were they supposed to get out, once the mission was done? She searched the local minds. What she found was not reassuring. If they failed, the bomb would detonate, triggering the eruption of the volcano, and they would be vaporized along with everyone else there. Which might be just as well, because the rest of the world would suffer horribly before being wiped out by the poison. If they succeeded, they would quickly vacate the mountain, because the eruption was building regardless. There was a hidden speedboat that would take them to Crete, where they would contact the authorities to arrange transport home. Assuming the animen did not discover the boat first. If so, they were on their own. Like all jury-rigged plans, this one was not completely tight.

"I agree," she said after a moment. "But what happens if we don't risk it?"

"Mankind dies."

She nodded. "So it's a choice between a bad risk, or outright doom."

"I hate your logic."

Brookstone appeared. He opened his mouth. "Yes, we'll go to Thera," Lavender said with resignation.

The man paused, taken aback. Then he remembered her telepathy, and wondered irrelevantly whether she had been with him that way when he used the head. She was tempted to tell him yes, though she hadn't been; she wasn't much interested in how men peed. "Uh, thank you," he said. "This way."

The teleporter was a disappointment. There were no fancy futuristic dinguses, no flashing strobe lights, no mysterious symbols. It was just a small empty chamber. The operative machinery was outside, all around it, focusing on the inside. There was barely room for the two of them. Barely was the word; they had to doff their clothing, because the animen were unclothed and apparel of any kind would give them away. "Aren't we cozy," Lavender said as he put his arms around her bare body.

"Yeah. I wish—"

Which was the trouble with males. In the presence of female nudity, their thoughts were limited to a single subject. "After the mission is safely over. Then I'll cool my core."

"Great!"

There was a *zzapp!* and they were in a dark tunnel, part of the labyrinth made when the animen were planting the poison. They unclasped, stood, and looked around as well as was feasible. The darkness was not complete.

"The action is that way," Lavender said,

pointing.

"Someone's coming." He was picking up on the footfalls.

"A wolf man and a cat man," she said, reading their minds. "They don't like each other much, but they're on the same team. They're running to reinforce the ones fighting the human troops."

"We'll join them."

"Neither knows anything about the bomb. But their leader may."

The two animen loomed out of the darkness. Both were fully furred and roughly human in outline, but had canine and feline facial features, pricked ears, and tails. "Where's the action?" The Bull called. "We're lost."

"Down ahead," the wolf man answered. "We're going there."

"You're speaking English," the cat man said.

Oops. This was Europe; English was their second or third language. "We're from the Brit contingent," The Bull said. "We got separated."

They were doubtful. Then Lavender spoke. "We liked each other's looks and we may not see each other again, considering the danger of this mission. We paused alone for just a few minutes, thinking it no harm. And took a wrong turn getting back."

Now the animen saw that she was emphatically female, her light fur not concealing anything. They were interested.

"There's no time," Lavender said.

The animen agreed, regretfully. "After this—" the wolf man said.

"Maybe," she replied, though "never" would have been more accurate. He needed to find himself a bitch—a female wolf—instead of a cow. Lavender's femininity was distracting them from questioning her identity. Maybe it would help with others.

They ran on to the action. There in a chamber were half a dozen other animen. "Reinforcements? About time you get here," a rhino man said. His epaulets, tacked to his thickly creased hide, indicated he was an officer. "The humans have lasers. They're messing us up. We need shields, not more bodies."

Lavender read his mind. He was a group leader. He knew about the bomb! It could be switched off. It was a manual lever beside the control panel, there in case of emergency complications. But where was the panel?

Rhino paused. "You and you," he snapped at The Bull and Lavender. "You're foreign."

"Brit contingent," The Bull said quickly.

"There *is* no Brit contingent. You're spies!"

Oops. The minds of the other seven authentic animen were focusing. "Flee!" Lavender told The Bull.

But the enemys' reactions were as fast as their own, and so was their strength. Four of them grabbed The Bull's arms and legs. He gave them a good fight, but couldn't get away. He was surprised, though he shouldn't have been; he had met his physical match.

The other four grabbed Lavender. She struggled, but was also overpowered. "Talk, cow girl," Rhino said. "Or we'll punish you."

"Punish her anyway," the wolf man said eagerly.

"Last chance," Rhino said. "Who sent you? What's your mission?"

Lavender couldn't break free of them. All she could do was turn lava and melt into hot glop. But that would take minutes. Her mother Lava could do it in seconds, but Lavender was only half volcanic. "No."

"Do it," Rhino told the wolf man. "Make her talk."

The wolf man turned the arm he held over to the cat man, while the other two animen held her legs apart, pinning her to the floor sunny side up. The wolf man came down on her, knowing better than to try to kiss her. Her mouth was not his object anyway. He oriented on her nether section.

"Don't!" she cried. Her change was way too slow.

He paused. "You ready to talk?"

"No!"

"Good." He set himself and thrust.

Lavender couldn't escape them, but she was already hot from her effort to melt. She heated her core further.

"Ooooo!" the wolf man howled as the smell of scorched flesh spread out. He scrambled back to his feet. The odor was coming from him as he danced about in agony.

The other animen stared. "Look at that!" the cat man said. "Roasted!"

"She's no animan!" Rhino said.

"That's right, I'm not," Lavender agreed. "I tried to warn you off."

"She's even hotter inside than outside," a gorilla man said, awed.

Rhino had had enough. "Kill her!"

But she was finally hot enough. The others let go of her arms and legs as their hands were burned.

She wasn't through. She got to her melting feet and walked splashily to where the four were still holding The Bull. "Let him go," she said.

They did not. So she put her melting hands on their arms, making their flesh sizzle. Now they let go.

But she could hardly walk, let alone run. "Pick me up," she told The Bull. "Don't touch my limbs."

He obeyed, putting his arms under her torso. That was hot too, but not enough to burn him. Yet. He carried her away from the staring animen.

"Where to?" he asked.

"There are old lava tubes honeycombing this mountain. That's what they adapted for the passages. We need to get into one the animen don't know about."

Behind them Rhino was organizing a posse. They would be in pursuit in moments.

"Where?"

She extended her mind, reading the mountain like the mind of a volcano, which it was. "There," she said, pointing up. "Knock a hole, jump in, close it over."

He set her down, reached up, and bashed the roof of the tube. A section broke off. "Toss me up," she said.

He took hold of her by the neck and groin and heaved. That wasn't the way a man should ordinarily handle a woman, but she wasn't hurt and it did the job. She sailed into the hole and landed beside it. Then he jumped up after her. He slid the fragment back to mostly cover the hole, and Lavender used her burning hands to melt the edges so they sealed. It was haphazard, but with luck, the animen wouldn't think to look *up* as they charged along the tube.

They didn't. They ran right on past in hot pursuit of nothing. The Bull and Lavender were safe for the moment.

But the hue and cry was after them, and they still had their mission to complete. How were they going to reach the control panel and turn off the bomb?

Chapter 10:
Lava Army

"How long until the bomb goes off?" I asked.

"Hang on," said Lavender and closed her eyes. One neat trick I had was that I could mostly see in the dark. Not always perfectly. But often good enough. Who knew bulls had night vision?

We were still in the lava tube. Reverberating through the stone, I heard the occasional explosion and what I thought was gunfire. There were still soldiers out there fighting the animen. What side was winning, I didn't know. That Villainous had been concocting this plan was obvious. One didn't lightly go about planting a nuclear warhead deep within an active volcano. This needed time and manpower, let alone securing an actual warhead. Next, he, or someone close to him, clearly had something to do with the animen.

And with me, I thought grimly.

There was a grand plan here, something that

had been hatched out for years, if not decades, and it was going down before our very eyes. Of course, Villainous and his crew hadn't considered Lavender, our ace in the hole so to speak.

"Okay, I found one of the minds that knows... we have less than thirty minutes. The animen are in a desperate fight. They had not expected human soldiers to be here. They thought they only needed to guard the volcano from a safe distance. They are trying to flee before the bomb goes off and subsequent eruption."

I knew, of course, that the soldiers were here as a direct result of Lavender's gifts. "Can you reach out to him?" I asked. "Convince him to switch off the bomb?"

"Maybe," she said and closed her eyes again. "Doubtful," she reported. "He's been trained to go down with the ship, so to speak. All the animen here are fully aware that this might be their last mission."

"Is there perhaps another, weaker mind we can influence?"

"I've never tried to influence anyone—"

"Then we have less than a half of an hour alive together, Lavender. When the bomb blows, we will die as surely as they will. I'm just half bull, not built to survive explosions. And your half human side could not endure a thermonuclear explosion, let alone a volcano blast."

She took my hand, and I yelped. She was still warm, but I powered through. If she wasn't able to convince someone to stop the bomb, then this might very well be my last physical contact...

"Get your mind out of the gutter," said

Lavender, and gave me a shot with her sharp elbow.

"Oof," I said, and grinned.

She had closed her eyes again, and was clearly stretching her telepathic skills to the maximum. Ten seconds later, she shook her head. "No one has second doubts about the mission. All are willing to die for Villainous."

"How many of them are there?"

"Dozens. Maybe a few dozen. Enough to thwart the soldiers. And all the animen are heavily armed as well. This was a well thought out scheme. The fighting is ferocious, but the animen have dug in. No one is close to the warhead."

My internal clock suggested we had inside twenty-five minutes, maybe less.

"Less," said Lavender. "My current contact is synched with the bomb. Twenty-four minutes and counting."

I paced the cramped lava tube. I was feeling a strong need to bust out and do some damage. I might get two or three of the animen, maybe more. As strong as I was, I suspected the rhino man was even stronger.

"Brute force isn't going to stop the bomb," said Lavender.

"You can communicate with the volcano," I said, pausing in front of her. My great horns scraped across the rock wall, causing a small amount of obsidian to break free and cascade around her.

"Yes, and watch it, will you."

"We're going to have bigger problems than just a handful of falling rock," I said. "Explain this: how was it possible that the volcano was amenable to this intrusion?"

"The planting of the bomb and army?"

"Right?"

"Unless the mountain is worshiped and revered, they are generally not too concerned with the goings on with man."

"You mean, it was probably unaware of what was happening."

"Probably. These are old souls, ancient beyond comprehension. Even if he blows and man is wiped off the face of the earth, what is it to him?"

"But you are, in a sense, one of his kin. Would he be so amenable to seeing you die, too?"

She considered as I continued to pace. "No. You're right."

"Perhaps we can appeal to him."

"And do what?" asked Lavender.

I continued pacing, and continued scraping free more rock. "Your mother was an extension of the volcano, was she not?"

"She was."

"And the volcano could form any shape it wants?"

"It can. I can, too—but not as quickly—"

"No time for that," I said. "What if the mountain formed not just one person, but an army of soldiers. Or whatever it thinks is fit to stop the animen?"

"Worth a try," said Lavender, and she closed her eyes again. I watched as her bottom melted into the floor, becoming one with it, so to speak.

I continued to pace...

Lavender's lips moved and I could see she was

communing with the volcano. Perhaps it was a sort of uncle to her. I didn't know.

I continued pacing...

"It is done, Bull," said Lavender. "But the volcano requires a sacrifice."

"Where are we going to find a virgin—"

"Volcanoes quit requiring virgins centuries ago. No, it wants a mate."

"What kind of mate?"

"The way my father mated with my mother. It desires such companionship."

"How will we find it a mate? There's no time —"

"Not now, silly. When this is all over. I agreed to the deal."

"Fine, so what do we do?"

"We don't do anything. He's forming the army as we speak."

"Then we need to get to the bomb. Do you know where it is?"

She closed her eyes, then nodded. "I do."

"Great," I said, and used my indestructible horns to break through the sealed entrance into the tube, and we dropped down.

Lavender led the way.

Chapter 11:
Aniwomen

They rounded a curve, going toward the control room where the bomb switch was. The route was not direct, because the lava tubes were not straight; they curved like spaghetti. Fortunately the fighting was no longer right here, and Lavender could sense the minds of any animen who happened to be in the vicinity. It should not be hard to avoid them by shifting to another tube.

"Not so fast, deary."

Lavender and The Bull both slewed to a stop. The creature before them had horns and fur and a great barrel of a chest under a tight blouse. But it was not exactly an animan in a skirt. It was an aniwoman. Lavender had been tuning only into male minds, so had missed this. "Oh!" At the moment she could not think of a more appropriate comment.

"Yes, I'm a buffalo gal," the woman said. "Rhino sent me. You won't be burning off any of my appendages, lady lava."

The Bull resumed motion. "Get out of the way, cow," he snapped as he strode toward her.

"Or what, horn head?" Buffalo inquired, swerving to intercept him. She caught him in her embrace and drew him in close for a bosomy hug.

Lavender saw that he was at a loss, not designed by nature to fight a female, especially one as phenomenally endowed as this one was. He was not about to hit her or hurt her. That was one reason Lavender herself had been able to manage him. Buffalo knew his incapacity and was using it against him. In a moment she would have him seduced or unconscious. Or both; it was in her mind, and she was a lusty creature.

Fortunately Lavender was made of different stuff, literally. "Or I will deal with you," she said. "I'll burn your ponderous udder."

"I think not, hot box," Buffalo said as she tightened her grip on The Bull. "Look behind you."

Lavender knew it before she looked. There were two more aniwomen: a tigress and a wolf bitch, both in roughly human form but with fur, tails, and catlike and wolflike faces. Both were quite well endowed in the human fashion, and wore almost translucent blouses and quite tight short skirts. She did not need to read their minds to tell their normal roles in the animan army.

Oh, damn! She might quickly handle one, but it would take time for two if she could do it at all. Worse, she saw that they were ready for her: they wore fireproof mitts. Rhino had learned well from his own encounter with her. She would not be able to come to The Bull's aid; she had problems of her own.

They gave her no time to consider. They pounced on her, each grabbing an arm with their mitts. Meanwhile The Bull, having to deal with Buffalo Gal on his own, was not doing well. She was squeezing against him and kissing him. He had always been a sucker for a kiss, and she was close to his own species. That kiss was clouding his male bovine mind.

Lavender knew she needed help. *Thera!* she called to the volcano. *Send a liquid lava rivulet here immediately!*

She felt the volcano's acquiescence. He was diverting an existing flow into this tube. It would arrive in minutes. Thera by himself was not smart in the human manner, but now he was attuned to her.

Meanwhile, Lavender had to prevent the two aniwomen from demolishing her, and the third from finishing The Bull one way or another. There was one advantage to being the center figure in a threesome: leverage. She was anchored in a manner they were not. She brought her arms forward, hauling the two along so that they collided with each other. They had the wit not to let go, so she hauled them back, and crashed them together again, harder. This time their heads banged, and they did let go, uttering feline and lupine curses.

Lavender jumped to tackle Buffalo Gal, clapping her hot hands to the aniwoman's sensitive ears. Buffalo snorted and turned The Bull loose. But now the other two aniwomen caught up, and it was three against one. Two grabbed her arms again, and the third made ready to gore her in the torso. She could not really be hurt this way, but it was taking invaluable time.

But now the lava flow was arriving. It was as yet only a thin trickle, but it would do. Lavender used her arms against theirs to haul herself into the air, kicked out with her legs, and hooked their legs so that the four of them crashed to the floor in a clumsy tangle.

Right onto the lava flow. It didn't hurt Lavender, of course, but it scorched the tails of the aniwomen. Maybe more than the tails. The stench of burning flesh puffed out. There was instant, fiery chaos.

Lavender drew herself free of the thrashing mass, snatched up a loose mitt, and used it to grab The Bull's arm. "Run!" she cried.

They ran while the three beast women struggled to get out of the lava stream without burning themselves worse. It was thin, but now it covered much of the floor. They literally could not stand on it. *Thanks, Thera!* Lavender thought, grimly amused.

Just find me a female with a spirit like yours, lava lady, he replied.

She intended to, when the time came.

They reached the bomb enclosure. But it was sealed off by a solid metal door with a similarly solid internal lock. The Bull tried bashing at it, but it was proof against his strength.

"I will melt the lock," Lavender said, discarding the mitt and heating her hands. Only five minutes remained.

Wait. The bomb had not been on a timer. It was set up to detonate when burning lava touched its mechanism. That lava was only five minutes distant. Yet it wasn't quite the same thing.

Thera! she thought. *Turn off the lava flow here!*

Soon. That was not because he didn't take her request seriously, but because liquid lava could not be cooled on a dime. It was going to be a close call. She'd better get in there and pull the switch, just to be sure.

"Well now, we meet again." It was Rhino. "I suspected you'd be canny enough to deal with the ladies, so I lurked here. Just as well."

And Lavender, distracted by events, had forgotten to scan for minds here. Rhino had outsmarted her.

The Bull charged him. The two collided with a thud that shook the tube. Then they fought. Rhino had no fear of The Bull; he was just as massive and tough and ornery. He knew that he did not need to overcome The Bull, just delay their effort long enough for the bomb to detonate. Rhino was quite ready to sacrifice himself and any other animen in the vicinity for the cause. Lavender had to grudgingly admire the animan's grit.

She did not go to The Bull's aid, because that would delay her effort with the lock. She focused on the mechanism, making her fingers as hot as only lava could be. The metal began to melt. But there was a lot of it, deeply set; would she melt out the lock in time?

Then she remembered something else. *Thera!*

Send some lava men here!
Soon.

The fight continued, as the two animen were evenly matched. Her melting effort continued. The minutes passed.

Three lava men burst into the chamber. They were only vaguely human, without proper faces or anatomical details; there had not been time to craft perfect ones. But they were animate and had arms and legs. They quickly carried Rhino away.

The three aniwomen arrived, having finally escaped the lava stream. Their bodies were badly burned in several places, but they were too tough to let that stop them. The lava men immediately took them on, and their female wiles were useless. So this battle had been won.

But the time was also up, and Lavender had not finished with the lock.

All of them froze, knowing that they might not exist seconds from now.

A minute passed. The bomb did not detonate. The key lava flow had been diverted or cooled enough. But the bomb was still armed, and could be set off at any time.

Lavender still needed to get in there and pull the switch to disarm it. But now there was a clamor of more animen charging toward the scene. This was bound to get complicated.

Chapter 12:
Shaft

"Oh no," said Lavender.

"What now?" I asked. I was facing the entrance into the chamber, an entrance from which I was expecting a small army of animen to appear at any minute.

"I just caught the last thoughts of Rhino before he went up in flames, literally."

Some of the animen had escaped, while others had fought the lava army to their deaths. Rhino had been one of them, and now the smell of cooked rhino flesh—along with cooked leopard and jackal —filled the chamber.

"Go on," I said. The sounds of running feet— and claws and hooves—were getting louder.

"The distant viewer the military used was wrong. The nickel plating over the weapon was only to protect the bomb from the lava. Lava doesn't melt everything; at least, not immediately.

Nickel has a melting point of—"

"Never mind all that, what's your point?"

"The bomb is still ticking, literally. And we have less than five minutes."

"Where's the shut-off switch?"

"There's no shut-off switch. The bomb is on a timer."

"Where is it located?"

"Not far from here, within an active lava tube."

I didn't know much, but I knew that most countries these days tested their weapons underground, where the damage was contained and fall-out was negligible. Just outside the entrance, I heard a commotion. Many more animen had arrived —luckily, they were met with just as many lava soldiers.

"You picking up my thoughts?" I asked Lavender.

"Yes. But even if Thera could cool the rock enough to completely encase the bomb, there's still a chance the explosion might set off the chain reaction Villainous is hoping for."

"How big is the bomb?"

"Not very big. A suitcase bomb, I think they call it. But big enough to possibly cause a volcanic eruption—hey, what are you doing?"

"Hop on up, cowgirl, you need to ride me out of here—and take me to the bomb."

"But what about the animen?"

"You let me take care of them..."

And with her superheated arms and legs wrapped around me, I charged out of the room, and heaven help anyone who got in my way.

***

Turns out, quite a number of animen and aniwomen had.

But when I have a full head of steam, there's not much on the planet that can stop me, even other animen. And I was charging through the lava tubes, horns and shoulders lowered, barreling and goring my way through. Amazingly, the molten soldiers let me pass. How they distinguished me from the enemy, I didn't know.

"They recognize me, you big oaf, now take a left into this next channel."

I did, turning and skidding, and then picking up speed.

"Turn here, and here."

I followed her directions until I found myself standing before a steaming pit that could have been the entrance into hell. Below, glowing magma churned and bubbled.

"It's down there," said Lavender, hopping off my shoulders, and joining me at the lip of the pit. Within the broiling pool of molten rock, I saw a smaller, darker section. An island of sorts, where Thera had cooled the lava around the nuclear device, back when we had thought cooling it would help. "This is the main conduit down to the large magma chamber. Most volcanoes explode when the pressure builds up inside this chamber, eventually blowing the top off a volcano."

"But there's no pressure in here now."

"Not yet. Truth is, no one knows what would

happen if a nuclear bomb went off inside a volcano. My guess—and Villainous's guess too—is that an explosion in here would blow the top off this volcano; in effect, mimicking an eruption."

"And blowing the poison into the upper atmosphere."

"Where it will be swept up and effectively spread far and wide." Lavender looked at me, and I saw the tears in her eyes. For the first time, I realized that this spunky woman who had suddenly appeared in my life, didn't know what to do, and didn't have all the answers.

I may not have all the answers, either, but I was a man of action.

"Contact Thera and have him—or it—continue to cool the surrounding magma."

Although nuclear weapons were often tested underground, I also knew that fusion bombs vaporized the surrounding rock, sometimes causing large craters to appear, or rock caverns that caved in on themselves. So, the more surrounding rock, the better.

"Look who's suddenly the expert," said Lavender, picking up my thoughts. "What are you planning to do?"

I scanned the vertical shaft that led to the vent above. It was hard to believe that just earlier in the day I was getting drunk in my living room... and now I was deep inside a volcano. "I'm going to plug up this hole and bury this weapon. We can't stop it from going off, but we can negate its effectiveness."

I was about to charge off, when I paused, swept Lavender up in my arms and gave her the mother of all kisses.

"It occurs to me," I said, breathing heavily, "that this might be the last time either of us are alive."

"Too bad we don't have another five minutes," she said, winking.

"Five? Give me two! Now, contact Thera and have him—"

"Already done, big guy, while you were busy kissing me. Is there anything I can I do?"

"You can stand back," I said, and then set off.

***

My plan was simple and bullish.

I lowered my head as I ran along the narrow shelf. My right horn—as hard as anything on earth—dug deep into the rock wall and plowed a deep furrow into the cylindrical shaft. The result was better than I could have hoped. Massive chunks of wall broke free, splashing down into the magma chamber below.

I continued running along the narrow shelf, once slipping and nearly losing my balance to plunge into the molten rock below. Anyway, I continued on, gasping, and digging my horn deep into the wall, leaving a wake of crumbling rock behind me.

By the time I had gone completely around the shaft, I was pleased to see the mayhem and destruction I'd caused. Much of the interior wall had crumbled down into the magma chamber, filling it, and, I hoped, burying the weapon deep below.

I paused only briefly to admire my handiwork —or my horn work—and swept Lavender up and onto my back.

And charged the hell out of there.

***

We felt the explosion.

The floor buckled and I buckled with it. I nearly lost my footing, but somehow managed to stay upright. I continued running, wondering when we would be vaporized too...

"Stop, Bull. We did it."

I slowed to a stop, gasping, hunched over. Some superhero I was.

"Thera has confirmed that the explosion has been contained. But he is badly wounded. Too wounded to think of a mate. I told him we would be back."

I nodded, too tired to speak.

"I've been thinking about Villainous."

"When... when did you have time to think about him?" I wheezed.

"Mostly during my piggy-back ride."

"Bull-back," I quipped, finally catching my breath.

"Did you find it strange that Mr. Brookstone appeared almost seconds after Villanous's media transmission?"

"He said he was nearby—"

"Or was he waiting?"

"He said his department had been keeping tabs on me."

"Why you? There are dozens of animen and aniwomen."

"Maybe they keep tabs on all of them. I just happened to be the closest."

"Fine. Then how is it that these other animen and aniwomen have formed an alliance with Villainous, leaving you out of it?"

"I've been entertaining the idea that he created them just for this purpose."

"Then that means he created you too. But how?"

"I thought I had been created by accident, one night while working as a rodeo clown. During a fluke lightning strike."

"Maybe it wasn't a fluke. Maybe the lightning strike had been pre-planned, for just that moment."

"But why?"

"Maybe you were his test subject. Maybe he got the wrong person. Maybe he had plans for you. Were you ever approached by anyone?"

"Not that I can think of? Just media types. Interviews."

"No one who asked you to join him?"

"No, not that I can think of."

She bit her lip, thinking. Her eyes glowed in the darkened tunnel, and I wondered if she could see into the dark as I can.

"I can, to a degree," she answered, although she sounded distracted.

"Maybe he hadn't gotten around to me," I said. "Maybe he was planning to come around. Maybe there are others like me—"

"No," she said. "I would have heard of them. The world would have heard of them. You were the rare fluke. You were the media sensation. Hell, I read about you in a magazine from my small island. I hadn't heard of the others."

"Which means he created them in secret," I said.

"But created you publicly," she added. "Why?"

"I don't know," I said. "I was just a down-and-out rodeo clown. Hell, I was a down-and-out superhero too."

Lavender began pacing. "Rhino and the others seemed brainwashed, somehow. Too willing to give up their lives for Villainous."

"What are you getting at?" I asked.

She paused, biting her lower lip. "I don't know. But you aren't like the others."

"Maybe I'm a fluke."

"Or maybe you are a mistake. Maybe you are the one animen who got away, so to speak. At least, got away from him. Maybe there's a reason why you were sent into this volcano. Lest we forget, Brookstone sent you here. Just like he appeared out of the blue."

"Or he is who he says he is, and I was sent here to help stop a global catastrophe."

"Oh, I have no doubt we foiled Villainous's plan. He certainly didn't expect someone like me to come along. The volcano *should* have exploded, and the poison *should* have been released into the atmosphere. It's just that you were supposed to die with it," she said. "Villainous wanted you dead. So did Brookstone."

I didn't like where this was going. Then again, I didn't like the idea of the entire human race being destroyed, either. I happened to like most of the human race.

"So what's the plan?" I asked.

"We get out of here... and talk to Brookstone."

Chapter 13:
Honeymoon

They had made the decision, but there were details to work out. Lavender knew they could not simply emerge from the volcano, catch a flight to America, and go to confront Brookstone. As far as Brookstone knew, they were now safely dead. If they tried to act openly, giving themselves away, they would soon enough be dead in reality.

"I have a problem with that," The Bull said.

"I am with you," Lavender said. "We need to stay dead, at least until we reach Brookstone."

"I always wanted to be a zombie," he said with a laugh.

"Not a zombie. They are undead. There's a difference."

"Or a ghost?"

"They lack substance."

"You can read my mind, but I can't read yours. What is on it, hotcore?"

Now she laughed. "I would cool my core for you, bovine boy. What I mean is that maybe we could assume different identities, so that we remain officially dead but are actually still in business."

"What identities?"

"That is the detail I am stuck on at the moment. Human folk like to have things like ID cards to prove they exist, and we can't use ours now. They also use money for things, and what we have isn't enough."

"Can the volcano help?"

"I'm not sure how, even if it were in good condition."

"Via the telepathic volcano network. To locate a couple of folk we might switch out with. Ones who maybe would like to have lava buddies like your mother or a really hot man."

Lavender was amazed. "You're a genius, bullhead!" She kissed him, her mouth now cool enough so as not to burn him. Then, answering his thought, she said, "No, it will take several hours to unheat my core. You'll just have to wait on that."

"Damn."

"Meanwhile, I'll ask Thera."

She reached out to the ailing volcano. Thera knew the score, from her mind, and agreed to contact other volcanoes in the area. They would survey the minds of all the thousands of tourists in the area.

"Meanwhile, let's get out of here," The Bull said.

They made their way cautiously up and out, avoiding any remaining animen. In due course they stood on the surface overlooking the waters of the Mediterranean Sea. The scene was deceptively placid.

A pair of figures approached them. Both The Bull and Lavender girded for mischief, until she touched minds with them. They were a lava man and lava woman, newly minted, both telepathic, sent by the volcano. They were coming to consult. "They're okay," Lavender murmured.

"Well now," The Bull said, eyeing the shapely nude female.

"Her core is hotter than mine," Lavender murmured, amused. "In fact, her surface would burn you. She's freshly made."

"Oh, I really wasn't thinking of anything."

The creature's mind laughter was so emphatic that even The Bull picked it up. "She's telepathic," Lavender reminded him. "She knows what you're thinking."

"Then tell her to put some clothes on," he said, embarrassed.

"They would burst into flame. Now let me dialog with them."

We have found a couple, the male thought.

"Found a couple!" Lavender repeated aloud.

"Damn!" The Bull said appreciatively.

The couple was John and Marsha, names they had chosen to mask their real intention, which was to exchange identities with a native couple on Crete. They were history buffs and wanted to explore the country at leisure. They had not been able to clear it with the authorities, so wanted to do it unofficially. In fact, they had married recently not from love, because they weren't each other's type, but their common purpose. They were on their honeymoon, pretending to be lovers while searching desperately for two Cretans who might want to exchange identities with them for a few months, visiting America. So far they had been unsuccessful, and the tour was almost over.

"Would they be amenable to associating with telepathic lava folk?" Lavender asked.

They might be. This wasn't certain, because the matter had not been raised with them. But if Lavender and The Bull talked with them, maybe there could be a deal.

"And do you lavas want to be making out with these humans?" The Bull asked. "They may not be perfect people."

What the lavas and the volcano wanted was full human engagement, from mind to genital, from joy to pain. Thera would experience the human mode completely, because of the mind contact; it wasn't even exactly vicarious. Just as Lavender's mother and grandfather had.

"We need to get to that cruise ship," Lavender said. "Soon."

"We'll swim," The Bull said.

"I'm not sure I am fit to swim. I can make the motions, but I'm pretty solid for my size and might simply sink. I wouldn't drown, but I wouldn't get there fast walking on the bottom."

"You'll ride my back."

"Good enough."

The lava couple did not try to swim for the same reason as Lavender. They would wait on the mountain, and be in touch telepathically. It seemed that the range of one telepath contacting another was much greater than when they were reading the minds of non-telepaths. Their range was also greater than Lavender's because they were full lava folk, undiluted by human ancestry. If the deal was made, they would know from Lavender's mind, and arrange a rendezvous.

"And cool off," The Bull said. "I don't care who the man is, he'll need a cool core." He was surely thinking of the wolf animan's fate.

They read his mind and agreed to be cooling while waiting.

The Bull entered the water, and Lavender clung to his back. She had cooled considerably, but her surface remained warmer than the human norm. "No danger of getting cold in the water," he remarked. "Not while you've got my back."

"I've got it," she agreed, pressing her breasts against him.

"Now you're heating *me* up," he complained.

"As if you mind."

He swam where she directed, going for the cruise ship. It took time, but he moved well, and by dawn they spotted it. It was one of those multi-decked liners that looked like huge stacked sugar wafers. It was anchored at the moment, while parties went ashore for assorted tourist traps. The Bull simply took hold of the anchor chain and shimmied up it, carrying Lavender with him.

No one was on the deck, by no coincidence; Lavender had checked nearby minds before they left the water. They shook themselves dry and walked naked to the cabin where John and Marsha slept. Lavender knocked on its door.

A young man answered. He looked at Lavender's bare body. "Uh—"

"We came in response to your summons, John," she said smoothly. "You and Marsha are looking for a couple to switch places with. We are that couple."

The thought of protesting flickered through his mind. Lavender inhaled. The thought fled. "Come in."

Marsha was still in her nightie, sitting on the bed. She opened her mouth. "You're beautiful, Marsha," The Bull said, going to sit beside her. She closed her mouth. He was after all a lot of man.

"We need to return to America anonymously," Lavender continued blithely. "We are thought to be dead in the volcano eruption, and we prefer to leave it that way. We will be happy to take your places here, and assume your identities, at least until the tour is finished."

"How did you know about—?"

She inhaled again, stifling him. "I am telepathic. I read it in your minds. I am Lavender, part human, part volcano lava. We have an additional deal for you, if you are interested. There is a lava couple who would like a social and maybe romantic association with a human couple. The woman looks like me, only more shapely. The man looks like my friend The Bull there, only more handsome. Both are telepathic and eager to oblige in any manner you might desire. They also represent formidable protection from any thugs who might seek to harm you as you poke about the ruins. I can put you in touch with them now if you wish to verify this."

"You're talking magic," John protested. "That doesn't exist."

"Yes, magic. For this reason, we prefer that you keep our secret. Magic exists, but it is not politically correct. However, the proffered deals are real."

Now Marsha spoke. "We're interested. But we'd prefer to check out these lava folk before making any commitments."

"Open your mind, and the man will contact you mentally," Lavender said. The thing about mental contact was that it was inherently honest. Lying was impossible, and compatibility was either there or not there.

Marsha was dubious, but tried it. In a moment a look of wonder crossed her face. Then interest. Then passion. "Oh, I want to meet you, lava man," she breathed.

"About the lava woman who looks like you—" John said.

"Open your mind. You will know her when she comes."

John did. "Wow!"

"They will guide you to them," Lavender said. "You will need to rent a small boat to go pick them up. You will have to deal in cash only, so as not to give away your identities, but they will help you earn enough money to live on. Remember, they can read minds; that makes a difference both personally and when dealing with other people. They will be your loyal companions. All they want is your respect and love. Speaking as the child of a human/lava couple, I can assure you that you can trust them. And the volcano they represent." She knew she didn't need to say more, because the lava couple was already in touch. They *knew*.

Marsha stood and put on her clothing. She efficiently packed her bag, but left her purse for Lavender. "We are on our way."

"Our identities are yours," John said, handing The Bull his wallet. "You can reach us through the lava folk if there is need."

Then John and Marsha departed.

The Bull lay down on a bed. "I'm overdue for a nap," he said, and conked out.

Lavender didn't need sleep in the same way he did, but she was ready for a good rest. She lay down on the other bed.

They were on their way to America, anonymously. And Brookstone was in for an ugly surprise, in due course. And maybe they would succeed in learning what he and Villainous were really up to.

Meanwhile they were John and Marsha, a honeymooning couple. She would have to drill The Bull on compartmentalizing his mind, and on mentally being a man in the throes of love and sex, so that any telepaths they might encounter would be fooled.

She glanced at The Bull, sleeping. She doubted he would have a problem. He was already dreaming of her.

Chapter 14:
Villainous #2

World Media Transmission #2

Greetings, I am Villainous.

You are still alive. Congratulations. If not for the heroic and misguided attempts of a few individuals, you would surely be breathing your last. The poison needed only to be inhaled by a few of you, and would travel quickly to the rest. My calculations predicted 90% human and primate casualties within 7 days. 99% within 10 days.

A lot of death. A lot of mayhem.

I do have a back-up plan, of course. Every good criminal mastermind has a back-up plan. Or three.

No, do not hate me. I am merely ending your existence quickly, before you do it slowly. Thus giving the earth a chance to rebuild from the plague that was the human race. Yes, I used the past tense.

Your death is imminent.

I had tried to remove you quickly and painlessly. The poison—one of my own concoctions —would have put you all to sleep, to breathe your last in blissful slumber.

Now, well, now you are not so lucky.

Truthfully, I prefer method #2.

Yes, I am a monster, after all.

Prepare for your death.

Now, you burn.

Chapter 15:
Secrets

We were sitting in the cabin, eating enough for three men. Correction, I was eating enough for three men. Turned out, Lavender didn't need much food.

"What do you eat?" I asked.

"You don't want to know."

"Try me."

She was sitting on the corner of the bed, watching me. She had long since ditched her horns to blend in with the other, non-horned tourists, which is how she was able to score me my personal buffet. Myself, I wasn't so lucky. These massive horns weren't going anywhere. For now, or until it was dark, I was cabin-bound.

She got up from the bed and plucked the fork out of my hand. Yes, I use a fork—and utensils in general. I'm not a complete animal, after all. Lavender held the fork before her, and in no time flat the pronged utensil began glowing. Then it did more than glow, it wilted over her knuckles like a plucked flower. And what she did next, I'll never forget.

She crumbled the fork up into a superheated, glowing ball... and then popped it into her mouth like something a kid would buy at a candy shop. Except this candy had once been a metal.

"Alloy to be exact. Not the most satisfying of snacks, mind you, but it will hold me over until I find something more suitable."

"And what's more suitable?" I asked, suddenly aware that the only fork in my possession was presently down my girlfriend's gullet.

"Silver. Gold. Nickel. Titanium. Your high-end metals."

"Jesus, that could get expensive."

"I never said I came cheap."

"You can say that again. Now, could you fetch me another fork?"

She did, and when she returned, she said, "The boat is abuzz."

"I thought it was afloat."

"Very funny, Bull. Apparently, there was another Villainous transmission. He's threatening to burn the world."

"Burn how? More lava?"

"I doubt it. There's only one way that anyone could reach the entire world with fire."

I set down the fork. I suddenly wasn't feeling very hungry.

"You can't mean..."

"I do. Somehow, the bastard got a hold of not just one nuclear weapon. But my guess is a whole arsenal of them. Enough to destroy the world."

"And not just primates," I said. "Us included."

"Well, you. I could withstand a nuclear blast, as long as I'm not too close to it. Radiation would do little to me."

"And you know this how?"

"Call it a gut instinct."

"Let's hope you're right. But for the rest of us, we have to stop this bastard once and for all. He's beginning to bug me."

Lavender laughed, then snatched up my fork, heated it, wadded it up, and swallowed it down.

"Will you quit doing that?" I said, setting aside my plate.

"Hey, I figure I'm gonna need my strength."

"For what?"

And now I saw a different sort of smoldering. This time from deep within her irises. "Hey," I said. "Nice trick."

"It's no trick, big guy."

"But don't we have the world to save?"

"We will, in due time."

"But—"

And she shushed me by pressing those super-heated lips onto mine. I might have whimpered a little.

***

It was after, and I think I broke the bed. Oops.

"You might have broken me, too, big guy," she said, winking. Lavender could, of course, adapt her shape readily enough. Apparently not as fast as the pure lava men and women, but swiftly enough, especially as I myself was heating up. "My question is: did you have to bray like something wounded?"

"Oh, did I?"

"You did, and it was loud."

"It was also the first, um, time since, you know..."

"Since you turned?"

"Yes. I wasn't even sure I could. I mean, I suspected I could, but I also thought I would seriously hurt..."

"A normal girl?"

"Yes."

"Well, luckily I'm not normal."

"And luckily you came into my life."

"You can thank the article I read on you. Which gets me thinking about Villainous."

"Ouch."

"Fun time is over, big guy. You might just be the only guy who can defeat Villainous, which is why he sent Brookstone after you in the first place."

"To set me up?"

"I think so, yes. You were very much meant to die in that volcanic eruption. And, for all he knows, you really did die."

"Fine. But let's circle back to this 'I might be the only person who can stop Villainous' business. Why would you say that?"

"Because I'm beginning to think that he created you."

"You said that. You thought I might be his first."

"Yes, I had thought that. But I have been thinking about it ever since, especially when you finally got off me and were catching your breath—"

"Hey, I'm beginning to think I didn't do a very good job—"

"You were fine. Now, can we talk about saving the world... again?"

"Fine," I said, although I was suddenly not very fond of the word. "Why do you think I can stop him? I mean, I can stop just about anyone, but why do you think he wants me dead?"

"Because you were his mistake, Bull. Think about it. While he was busy building an army of animen and aniwomen, he inadvertently created you too. Not to mention, you were the one he couldn't control. Last I checked, you aren't doing his bidding, unless your bidding was bedding me."

"Very clever," I said. "Who knew lava girls could be so funny."

"Half lava," she said.

"Fine. So I was his big mistake. So what does that mean?"

"It means he fears you somehow. Enough to arrange to get rid of you in the volcano."

"Fears me why? I mean, if I ever see the little weasel, I'd wring his neck."

"No. It's more than that. Anyone with half a mind would fear your great size and strength. No, he fears something else."

"While we think about it, why don't you give me another shot at it."

"Shot at what?"

I jutted a thumb at the bed behind me.

"Oh no, big boy. I'm still recovering. I think my legs are still out of joint—oh, don't mope. No one likes a sad bull."

"I just think I could do better. I was a little rusty."

"You could say that again. But there's always later. Especially when the world isn't being threatened with nuclear destruction."

"Fine," I said, and sighed. Yeah, I was moping.

"There's something about you. Something he can't predict. Or something else." She suddenly paused, turned and faced me. She took my head in her hands. They were pleasantly warm. "I have an idea. No, not that idea. Another one. Let me search your mind... maybe there's something hidden in there... something I can find that you might not be aware of."

"Worth a shot," I said.

And with that, she closed her eyes, and I felt her probing my mind, probing deep...

Chapter 16:
Mark Twain

It was like walking through a wasteland or a garbage dump, this excursion through the guts of a man's mind.

It seemed that half of it was concerned with sex, a third with survival, and the rest with assorted things washed up on the shore of a frustrated existence. It didn't help that she was the passionate object of the sexual portion; both his man aspect and his bull aspect wanted to get into her and never get out. Completely unrealistic, of course, but the underlying passion had little concern for reality. If there was one thing men were stupid about, it was sex. Fortunately around the edges, among the weeds, were some reasonable constraints, such as the knowledge that she could heat her core and incinerate any intrusion she did not want. Also, the early throes of what could reasonably pass for love.

This bull's experience with that china shop was limited, but it was already forming into a ring in his nose.

What she was looking for was anything relating to Villainous or the animen, that predated the Villainous broadcast. The Bull had not consciously known of them, but they had surely known of him, especially if he had been created as part of the program. What was different about him? Why did they want to eliminate him? Just because he had a bovine mind of his own? That might be annoying, but not reason for such a complicated effort to get rid of him. Why hadn't they tended to the extermination of mankind first, then gotten around to the details like The Bull at their convenience? He really would have known nothing about the animen had Brookstone not told him. Not that ignorance would have been bliss, as the human realm collapsed.

There had to be something else. Something that made him a real threat to Villainous. How could that be, when he was just one of a group of conversions? It had to be a difference that set him apart from the others. Yet the merging of animal and man had been successful, so it wasn't physical. Could it be mental? It wasn't extraordinary intelligence; he was okay, but no genius. It wasn't any great background knowledge; he didn't know anything that had not already been in the minds of the man and the bull before they merged. He did not have any secret knowledge of Villainous scandal that could be used for blackmail. He simply didn't know anything outside of himself.

But there was an obscurity. It was like a passage into a cellar chamber marked NO TRESPASSING. What was that doing here? Why bother to mark it off? It was right between the mind of the bull and the mind of the man, like an interface. It was not native to either mind; it was something inserted from outside. That had to be the work of Villainous.

She oriented on it. It seemed like a connection between the two minds, except that it was closed, not open. Why have such a thing, when the minds were essentially unified without it? It seemed to be without purpose, and that made her suspicious. Why go to all the trouble to put it in there if it had no function?

Lavender had no real knowledge of the wiring of computers, but she had heard of something called a logic gate. As she understood it, which was hardly at all, it was a kind of arbiter of a concept, like a transistor that limited the flow of current along a wire, unless a signal to the transistor told it to get out of the way. This was blocking a concept, unless told to unblock it. What was the concept? All she could tell was that on one side was the bull mind, and on the other was the man mind. They were walled from each other, at least to this very limited extent.

She knew she was on to something. Since the man and bull minds were already working together well enough, so that their joint body could function and their joint mind could agree that they desired to have endless sex with a tough enough woman, why should just this one portion be limited? She traced the leads, and discovered that they led to the centers of identity: the innermost essence of the bull and the man, which remained separate. Their self-awareness. In fact, The Self, the seat of personal consciousness. That connection was blocked off by the logic gate. That meant that there was no community of identity in this one area. The identity was that of the human, while that of the bull was outside looking on. What would happen if the transistor was told to change and let the bull identity through?

She did not need to ponder long on that. The bull was raging; it wanted to dominate, and charge through the streets goring man, beast, and building, leaving a wake of destruction behind. If it ever got through and took over, beauty would be governed by the beast. The man she knew and was starting to love would be gone.

It was surely similar in every animan and aniwoman: the beast was chained, the human governed. But why? If the gate were ever changed, either the animals would take over, or the creature as a whole would become dysfunctional as its two selves fought over possession of the body. Why nullify the animen like that? Why have even the potential for nullification?

She left that question in abeyance as she studied the gate. Now she saw that this one was broken; maybe the lightning strike that merged bull and man had incidentally fried the gate. Either the bull or the man could have been given control; as it happened, it was the man. Maybe others had failed, and the raging animal had run amok and gotten itself killed. This one had been lucky. So if the signal came through to change the gate, nothing would happen; this one was off its hinges and would not move. The Bull was safe; he would never turn fully animal and destroy himself.

But, again, why? Obviously the dangerous gate had been installed for a reason. What could that possibly be?

The question brought its answer: animen were wild creatures, prone to violence. Only the human element made them at all manageable. Suppose one got out of control? A signal to the gate could shut it down in a hurry. Villainous might be justifiably paranoid about his minions; one on the loose could be very bad mischief. The Bull was proof of that. There needed to be a way to turn him off in a hurry, quietly so as not to disturb others in the vicinity. The gate would do it. The boss was making sure there could be no revolt of his minions.

Now she was beginning to understand. Villainous must have caught on that The Bull's gate was broken, so he could not be quietly turned off. Maybe Brookstone had verified that, when they met. So he had to be eliminated before he got troublesome. In fact, he was already troublesome; maybe the same broken gate accounted for his independence from Villainous and determination to be his own beast-man.

So what was the signal that would change the gate, not that it mattered in The Bull's case? This time she followed the lead from the gate. It went to the nerve center for speech and hearing. So it was a spoken command. What was it?

PIERS ANTHONY & J.R. RAIN

Finally she ran it down: Mark Twain. She knew that was the pen name taken by a famous American writer, Samuel Clemens, who had once worked on a riverboat on the Mississippi. When the water got shallow they had to know exactly how deep it was so the boat would not snag on a bar. They needed at least twelve feet clearance, or two fathoms. When the man called out "mark twain," that meant it was deep enough, but watch it. Certainly there were treacherous waters here!

Now at last she had it: when an animan heard those two words, the logic gate would open the channel for the animal, and internal hell would ensue. It was a ready way to nullify any or all of them.

She withdrew from The Bull's mind, carefully, trying not to disturb any of the muck or incite the sexual interest that lurked throughout. It was like backing out through a deep dark cave haunted by myriad ghosts. She had never been this deep in anyone's mind before, and hoped not to have to do it again soon, if ever. She felt like taking a shower. It wasn't just The Bull; she knew that plumbing this deep in any male mind—and maybe in any female mind too—would be like this. Minds were best left to their filthy privacy.

"I felt you tramping around in there," The Bull said. "Weird. What did you find?"

"I found the answer," she said. "Now I know why Villainous wants you promptly dead."

"Why?"

"There is a logic gate in every animan mind that—" She paused, picking up his blank response.

"It's like a stoplight at an intersection. The logic gate does for thoughts what the light does for traffic. It directs the flow so that there's no trouble. If the light malfunctions, such as by showing green both ways, the cars will crash and there'll be a mess, and that intersection will be blocked for hours."

"There's a stoplight in my head?"

"The equivalent, yes. If it receives the signal 'Mark Twain,' it will malfunction, and the man and the animal will struggle for control of the body. That's like crashed traffic."

"Who?"

"Mark Twain. It's the pen name for the American writer Samuel Clemens."

"Why didn't he use his own name?"

"Writers are odd. They like to use other names."

"They're ashamed of what they do?"

"No. At least I don't think so. The best ones use pseudonyms."

"But why?"

She was getting impatient. "You'd have to ask them."

"I mean why put the stoplight in my mind?"

Oh. She should have read his mind. "To put you out of commission."

"But—"

"Don't worry. Your stoplight is broken. It's locked on you regardless. Otherwise when I said the words, you would have gone kaplooey."

"Okay. So my stoplight's broken. Is that reason to kill me?"

"Oh, yes! Because it means Villainous can't control you. Worse, for him, you can put any other animan out of commission in a hurry, just by saying those magic words. In fact, we could broadcast those words across the globe and put any animan or aniwoman who heard them out of commission."

"But why wouldn't they wipe out mankind first, then come after me, since I'm only a detail?"

"Because even after mankind is gone, you could still wipe out any other animan with those words. And if you tell the human authorities those words now, you can bollix the whole animan campaign. Any human will be able to take out any animan just like that. So they need to take you out before you can do any such thing."

"But how do they know I know the words?"

"They don't. Yet. They want to kill you so you won't have a chance of learning them. Once they learn that you're still alive. That's why we need to stay dead as long as we can."

He nodded. "Okay. You can poke into my mind anytime, you marvelous creature. Just feeling you in there made me get ideas."

Didn't she know it! "Thanks, no. If we could take the sex out of your mind, there would hardly be enough left for you to function. But we do need to protect ourselves, to take out some insurance, because once they learn we're not dead, they will be totally committed to our extinction."

"Insurance?"

"Such as writing out the words and what they do and sending the letter to a newspaper to publish —if we die. Or maybe better, putting them into the

Internet with a logic gate triggered by our deaths. Maybe we'll have to send our own code words every few hours or it will send out the words anyway. So that Villainous will know that he can't simply rub us out. He will have to negotiate."

"I don't think he'll negotiate."

"Then we'll broadcast the words and wipe out his nefarious project."

He nodded again. "I like it. Now—"

She laughed. He really had never left his favorite subject. "Well, I guess I've been poking into you pretty intimately, so it's only fair to let you poke me in return. I wonder if I could wear out your sexual interest for a few hours so we could focus on more important things for a while."

"Not a chance."

"Why not?"

"There *is* nothing more important." Then he grabbed her, and she did not resist at all. She was ready for some diversion herself. She was already shoring up her torso and cooling her core for some serious interaction.

But she knew that their battle with Villainous was just beginning.

Chapter 17:
The President

Okay, now I *know* I broke the bed. In fact, it was little more than padded kindling at this point... with scorch marks, of course.

"Oops," said Lavender when she got up from the broken bunk. "I think I might have enjoyed myself more than I let on."

I grinned and noted the deep grooves in the walls, the punctures in the bedding, the knocked over lamps and dislodged sconces. I had even managed to tear up the carpeting. "John and Marsha are definitely getting a nasty letter from the cruise ship."

"I doubt they care," said Lavender, who had been too quick to don the terry cloth robe hanging in the bathroom. I had only been able to admire her backside for the briefest of seconds. "The cruise ship has insurance, and I'm sure the lava couple is keeping the pair of them busy. That is, if Thera has recovered enough from the explosion. And no more admiring my backside, or any side, until this business with Villainous is done. You do realize he threatened to scorch the earth, right? For all we know, the world is in flames while we've been canoodling."

"Oh, that wasn't canoodling. That was—"

"I know what it was, Cow Brain. My point is, we have to get serious about this threat. Villainous is not someone—"

"Or something," I cut in.

"—to take lightly. He's already proven himself capable of getting his hands on one nuclear weapon. What makes us think he hasn't gotten a whole arsenal at his disposal?"

"Because only a handful of countries had that capacity to blow up the world. No way in hell Villainous was also busy making enough nukes to blow up the world."

"Well, he was busy designing a new race..."

"Exactly. Too busy to also be in the bomb-making business. Besides, the United States has eyes everywhere. No way someone is making that kind of weaponry in secret."

"Then how else would he hope to torch the earth?"

I didn't know, but I just caught a peek of Lavender's robe opening—an opening that was promptly closed. Geez, that woman was in my head.

"No need to be in your head to see what you're leering at, Bull Boy. And I just had a thought."

"So did I..."

She ignored me. "Just because Villainous

couldn't have made the bombs, perhaps he has access to existing bombs."

"It would take a lot more than one suitcase nuke to incinerate the earth."

"Exactly. Like, say, all the nukes in the United States' arsenal?"

I laughed and nearly reached for the woman sitting at the edge of the broken bed. Or was it called a bunk? "Only the President of the United States can launch those nukes, don't you know? There are some serious safeguards in place. I read about it once. No one, but no one, can walk in there and launch those nukes."

"No one but the president," said Lavender, and she had a far-off look in her eye that had nothing to do with sex, but everything to do with mischief.

"What are you getting at, lava girl?"

"Villainous has already managed to place a high-ranking mole in the Department of Defense—"

"We don't know for sure if Brookstone is—"

"No, but it's likely. For now, let's assume he is."

"Or we can assume that Villainous is full of hot air, and the rigging of Thera was his best chance at world domination."

"And what if we're wrong? What if Villainous has one more trick up his sleeve?"

"Then we leave it to the people who can do something about it. Namely, the military. No way he's getting close to the nukes."

"He may not be... but the president can."

"Now, hold on—"

"Like I said, he already managed to get

Brookstone in—and for all we know, he's an animan himself. Maybe there's a cat tail curled inside his suit. My point is, he could be something smaller, less obvious than..."

"A bull?"

"Right."

"Do you know how crazy this is, Lavender? Are you suggesting that the President of the United States is an animan, too?"

"I'm not sure what I'm suggesting. But I am guessing that if Villainous could get to the president, he could get to the nukes...and that would be the end of it all."

I paced the small confines of the cabin. "Just craziness. You know that right?"

"Hear me out, Bull. Villainous has already proven to be a master geneticist. Hell, he created his own subspecies of man and animal. You're living proof of that. How much harder would it be for him to create, I dunno, a clone of the President?"

"A clone? Did you just say a clone?"

"I did, and I'm being serious. What if he had... and even now, this clone was about to replace the real President of the United States... What if, at this very moment, the president is being held captive in secret, while his clone is about to launch enough explosives to destroy this world many times over?"

"I would say I just made love to a crazy woman."

"There was no 'making love' about any of this," said Lavender, pointing to the destroyed furniture.

I stopped pacing and eyed the open laptop on

the desk. It had been left by John and Marsha. I knew what she was saying was ludicrous, but there was just enough doubt in me to sigh heavily and sit at the desk. "I saw on the news last night that the president was vacationing in the Mediterranean. On a heavily guarded and remote island. Not very far from us, in fact."

"Perhaps that's why Villainous chose Thera, knowing the president would be nearby, just in case the volcano eruption plan fizzled."

I didn't like this. I didn't like any of this. I especially didn't like the idea of knowing that life on planet earth might be destroyed, all because of one crazy bastard. "Fine," I said. "So what do you propose we do?"

Chapter 18:
Yot

Lavender's mind was spinning. She hated having to come up with world saving plans on the spur of the moment. In fact she hated having to do it at all. All she wanted was to settle down to eating, sleeping, and cuddling with a good man who was comfortable with her nature. Saving the world required too much thought and effort.

"I propose we warn the president, so that he can avoid the clone and not contribute to the end of the world as we know it." There; that was pretty simple, once she got it formulated.

"But he's thousands of miles away."

"No. I told you. He's nearby, on his yacht."

"Oh, yes. What's a yot?"

"A big pleasure boat. Y A C H T."

"Oh, a yaw-chet."

He had not made the connection between the sound and the spelling. He was an inland guy, unfamiliar with the fancy craft that came to the island she had been raised on. It wasn't worth a hassle at the moment. "Whatever."

"Isn't he surrounded by secret service men who won't let anyone get close to him?"

"Unless it is someone they already know about," she said. "So they let him through."

"If we have trouble reaching him, wouldn't the clone have trouble too?"

"Good question. Maybe they sneaked the clone into his bathroom, and when he goes there to defecate—"

"To what?"

"Poop. Something you fully living folk do a lot of. The clone can be waiting there, and take his place, and the secret service folk may never know the difference. So what we need to do is get to that bathroom first, and take out the clone. Then he'll be able to poop in peace."

"Does he know about us? So they'll let us in?"

"I don't think so. We're largely anonymous, by design. But maybe—" She trailed off, an idea coming to the fore.

"Maybe what?" he demanded impatiently.

She silenced him with a kiss as she focused on the elusive thought. It related to the volcano. On the way the two lava figures had connected to John and Marsha. Something about that had differed from the way she related to The Bull. They were telepathic, yes; so was she. So that wasn't it.

The Bull managed to free his mouth. "But—"

She kissed him again, harder, and goosed him for good measure. The lava folk's telepathy reached farther than hers, because they were first generation magma, while she was diluted second generation. She could do what they could, but slower and not as well. Even so, there was something—

He escaped again. "What—"

She pushed him down on the battered bed, tore open the front of her robe, whipped out a hot breast, and jammed it against his face. She held him tightly in place so he couldn't breathe, let alone interrupt her thinking. He hardly struggled at all; he liked breasts and he could hold his breath for a long time. His body relaxed. Better yet, so did his mind. He liked keeping abreast of the situation.

What were they doing that she was not? How did it relate to the present challenge? They had reached out to John and Marsha to reassure them—

Now he was licking her nipple. It was ticklish. She suppressed her reaction and held firm.

And there it was. The lava folk had not merely read the human minds, they had projected their own thoughts, so that John and Marsha got to know them in a hurry, from the inside out. Lavender couldn't do that; all she did was read minds.

And he was sucking. Okay, that was distracting. She bore down harder, filling his mouth with more of her breast. She doubted he could take the whole thing in, but he was trying.

Yet wasn't she lava too? Diluted, but still a child of the volcano. If they could project, why couldn't she?

She reached out to the lava couple, questing, hoping they would read her. *How do you project?*

The answer came immediately. *Like this.*

Suddenly the ability was in her mind. It was

indeed like this. She had had it all the time, but somehow never thought to invoke it. It was not as strong as theirs; she would have to touch a person physically to project a thought into his mind, at least until she knew him. But she could do it.

Thank you! she projected. She could do it long distance, with a lava person, because they had minds like hers, only more so.

Welcome, the female thought. She was in a rather intimate clinch at the moment, having cooled her core, but her mind was free.

Marsha's fun, the male thought. *But your breast notion is fun too. I will ask for hers.*

"Welcome," Lavender murmured, laughing. She pulled her own breast out of The Bull's mouth. "I need to save some of that for myself, before you swallow it whole," she told him, tucking it back into her gown.

Now he could talk. "What—?"

"I will project to the secret service folk I encounter," she said. "Reassuring them that I'm legitimate. And when we get to the president, all I need is to touch his hand, to familiarize myself with him. Then I will be able to project the danger. To warn him about the clone. So he can protect himself."

"Okay." He did not understand the details, but was satisfied that she had worked out the program.

They got on it immediately. They donned swim suits, borrowed tourist scuba diving gear from the cruise ship inventory, fitted it on, and dropped into the sea. They were headed for the president's "yot," only a few miles away. Lavender didn't actually need the gear to breathe, but the fins did help her swim without sinking. So did the little paddle motor. Mainly it was camouflage: they needed to resemble innocuous tourists diving for shells.

Their minds, too. Just in case there was an enemy telepath in the vicinity. *Remember,* she thought to him. *We are the honeymooning couple John and Marsha, and all we have on our minds are love, sex and shells.*

Got it, he agreed, not thinking to be surprised by receiving her thought. Maybe he didn't fully realize that it wasn't his own thought. Then: *shells*?

We're shell diving. It's what tourists do when they're not in the bedroom.

He considered that. *How about underwater?*

He was not thinking of shells. *No. We don't want to tear up the Mediterranean the way we did the cabin.*

Oh. He was of course disappointed, but also flattered by the implication that their lovemaking could tear up the seascape. Men—what could you do except love them?

They swam toward the president's boat. Lavender ranged out with her mind, seeking animen. She found some scattered around, but they were neither telepathic nor thinking of her. They could be bypassed and ignored.

Closer to the craft there were straight human lookouts, actually secret service personnel, male and female, routinely scanning for any potentially hostile craft. None were looking under the water.

They made it to beneath the "yot" without raising any hue and cry. So far so good. Were she in charge of presidential protection, she would damn well be scanning underwater too; it was sloppy. Maybe the ones assigned to do that were off having a wild party with call girls and all. The secret service had a reputation to maintain, after all.

It was dusk. *No one's watching aft*, she thought to The Bull. *We can climb the anchor chain, same as before.*

They did, The Bull carrying her over his shoulder, gear and all. They made it to the deck. So far so good, again. She doffed her fins, set down her motor, and scanned and located the president alone in the master cabin. Actually they didn't need to approach the president himself, just the lavatory (interesting word) to take out the lurking clone. Because there was indeed a presence there.

"Freeze!"

They froze. Men appeared from their hiding places. "Oh, crap!" The Bull muttered. "It's a trap."

So it seemed. But why hadn't she located the men mentally? She had been scanning constantly.

Then she remembered what Brookstone had said: compartmentalization. They had walled off what they were really doing, and she hadn't thought to check all the compartments. She had been an idiot.

Worse, some of them were animen, who had been similarly hidden. Damn! Now they stood in a circle around the two of them, and they were armed. Any false move would make them pile in.

Armed? As she checked their minds more closely she realized that there were no guns here, only knives or other weapons. And she knew why:

the president's wife had forbidden firearms on the "yot." More power to her! But that did not mean that these men were not formidable.

All she could do now was to try to alert the president openly. "We have to see the president," she said loudly. Though she did not move physically, she was busy both heating her core for action and enlarging her breasts and hips to make a sexier presentation in the tight wetsuit. Every little thing could make a difference, especially when dealing with men.

The head man gazed at her evenly. "Why?"

It was clear there would be no reasoning with him; his mind showed it. Also, these men were under orders to capture the intruders alive. Why? The men did not know, but would obey to the best of their ability. The leader, appreciating her growing sexiness, hoped to get to rape her the moment it was allowed. He did not understand her full nature. She was going to enjoy burning him to a crisp.

Now she realized also that there had to have been a telepath involved. Just as she had been scanning mentally for animen, the telepath would have been scanning for her, while remaining out of her mental sight. So her arrival with The Bull had been no surprise, and they had walked blithely into the trap. It was a lesson for the future, if there was one: learn to detect any telepathic scanning that touched her.

But now they had to act.

To the president's cabin, she thought to The Bull. *Now!*

Then she said aloud: "Mark Twain."

The animen stood unmoving, fighting their internal battles. They were out of the fray. That reduced the odds at the outset.

Meanwhile The Bull leaped into action so swiftly that even these trained men were caught off guard. His horns and fists hurled them left and right. Meanwhile, Lavender simply charged forward, picking up the squad leader and flung him overboard. He had not anticipated anything like that from this pretty girl with the swelling bosom. Her core power was stronger than any man or woman's. Another reason she was a good fit for The Bull.

A man emerged from the president's cabin. It was the president himself! She knew him from his pictures on the media.

"Mister President!" she cried. "You are in great danger!"

"Oh, I doubt it," he said, eyeing her torso.

"Do not go near your bathroom—"

She broke off, reading his mind. They were too late.

This was the clone.

Chapter 19:
Submersible

"Mr. President," I said, not sure what the protocol here was. I almost reached out for his hand, then nearly bowed. In fact, I did a little of both. No doubt looking foolish.

"Give it a rest, Horny," said Lavender. "He's a fake."

The faux president bowed. "I would say all the way down to my fingertips, but that's not quite accurate, for even a clone's fingertips will vary from the original. But everything else is nearly identical."

"All of which will help you launch the nuclear weapons," said Lavender.

The clone bowed. Lord, but he looked just like President Walton. "But how?" I asked. "President Walton was only elected, what, three years ago? How could a clone exist so quickly? I mean, don't they have to, you know, grow up?"

Lavender turned to me. "We really don't have time for this, Bull. I've scanned the clone's mind, and I can ascertain he's only a few years old. In fact, barely over a year."

"I don't understand—"

"You can thank Villainous's advances in technology for that. Not only has he perfected cloning humans—which isn't that difficult to do—but he has created the ability to do so quickly. The clone before us has limited intelligence. In fact, he knows only what he has been trained. Correction. He is being operated by a distant mind."

"What the devil does that mean?"

"He's being remote controlled."

"I need a beer."

"Focus, Bull," said Lavender. "You can drink later, when all of this is over."

"And if we survive."

"That goes without saying," said Lavender. "First things first, we need to know where the real president is. You," she said to the fake. "Where are you keeping President Walton?"

"I don't answer to you, bitch."

"No, you don't. And your mind is blank. Bull, throw him in the ocean. Feed him to the sharks."

"With pleasure," I said, and picked him up by the scruff of his neck, feeling an odd sense of fear and guilt grip me. After all, he looked so much like the real president. At the railing, I paused. "Are we sure he's a fake?"

"I'm sure."

"Then here goes."

"Wait!" screamed the fake.

"Wait for what?" asked Lavender, who came up to my side. Behind her, I heard growls and gnashing of teeth, and claws clamoring over the wooden deck. The animen, who had been out of earshot before, were more animal than men, and they were fighting it out on deck. I don't know how Noah did it.

"The clone knows nothing," he said, in a voice that suddenly sounded a little higher pitched. "Please put him down."

"Do no such thing, Bull," said Lavender. "Who are we speaking to?"

There was a short pause. The man weighed close to two hundred pounds. For me, that might as well have been next to nothing. I could hold him over the railing all day if I had to.

"I am Villainous," said the voice through the faux president.

"You are controlling the president?" asked Lavender.

"I control many of my creations."

"You don't control The Bull," said Lavender.

"No, and that is unfortunate. He ended up being a real pain in the ass."

"Hey," I said.

"Where's the president?" asked Lavender. "The real president?"

"He's needed elsewhere. The clone is just for show, of course. His fingerprints or retinal scan won't unlock the nuclear codes. Only the real president can launch a nuclear attack. And he will, too, whether he wants to or not."

Elsewhere on the ship, I heard crashing and

growling and the sounds of feasting. The animen were really going at it. A part of me wanted to jump in there, and join the fray. The animal part of me, that is.

Lavender put a hand on my arm. "I scanned the ship. The secret service agents are being held below decks. Many of them are wounded. The one I have connected to understands that before the nuclear bombs can be launched, the president must be positively identified. The United States has a two-man rule in place, and while only the president can order the release of nuclear weapons, the order must be confirmed by the Secretary of Defense."

"You are a powerful telepath, my dear," said the fake president dangling from my grip. "I could use you."

"For what?" asked Lavender, surprising me.

"To help rule our new world."

"There won't be much of it left once the bombs go off."

"Not much above ground, dear girl. But I am building a Utopia below. Far, far below, where it will be safe, and where your kind will thrive."

"My kind?"

"Yes, Lava girl."

"And what of the humans?" she asked, surprising me further. I sure as hell wished I could dip into her mind to see what she was up to. But she was the telepath. I was just the muscle.

"They will be removed, of course. Humans are a plague to this earth."

"And yet you propose to wipe the earth clean of all life, not just humans."

"Like a forest fire consumes the dead log, a nuclear holocaust will give the earth a chance to renew."

"In thousands of years," said Lavender.

The president continued dangling over the railing of the ship. He had given up fighting me and now hung there, watching Lavender with interest.

"Oh, it will be more than a thousand. But what's a few thousand years to this planet? Once the radiation has decayed, life can begin anew. As we watch from below."

"And you will be dead many times over."

The president laughed in my hands, sounding just like the real president. So weird. "My dear, I have created life. I have created new species. What makes you think I haven't conquered death as well? Everyone in my world will live for as long as they wish. Reborn over and over again into fantastic new bodies. Stronger bodies. Join us, Lavender."

"I'm interested," she said, and I turned and stared at her.

She looked at me and shrugged. "We should at least hear the guy out."

"You mean, just before he kills us?"

The president laughed in my arms, following this conversation. And for all I knew, Villainous was following my thoughts too, and Lavender's. Which meant...

Which meant the bastard was nearby.

"Of course I'm nearby, Bull," said the president. "Now, if you'll put me down, you'll find a submersible on the starboard side of the ship. Yes, that means the other side of the ship. You missed it coming in from the port side of the ship. You will find your president in there."

"And you too?" asked Lavender.

"Of course. We've been waiting for you."

Chapter 20:
Templa

Lavender thought fast, doing her best to shield her thoughts from the telepath she knew had to be close by, maybe with Villainous. But she needed more. Maybe The Bull could help.

"Grab my ass," she murmured to him.

"Huh?" He knew she wasn't naive about his interest, but she had always discouraged public displays of it.

"Now."

He was confused, but happy to obey. He put down the clone and took hold of her right buttock and squeezed. His mind plunged into a maelstrom of sexual aspiration.

"You must have an interesting personal relationship," the clone said, licking his lips. The sight made him wish for something similar. He was, after all, male. They were like cookie cutters in this respect.

"Yeah," said The Bull. "She's some doll."

Now there was so much sexual tension that any telepathic contact with their minds should be hopelessly compromised. That and her shield should suffice for long enough.

Lavender sent a thought to the two lava folk. *Vital message.*

Transmit.

"Mark Twain stops animen." *Send it to all volcanoes, to tell humans, unless I tell them not to every 24 hours.*

Done. They did not question her meaning or her reasoning, knowing from her background mind that this was serious business.

That was it. *Thank you.*

She returned to the immediate scene. "Now let go," she murmured.

The Bull reluctantly obeyed, knowing that she had her reasons in this department too. The sexual tempest eased.

"I presume there was a point to that little display," the clone/Villainous said.

Now it could be told. "Yes. To block out your telepath while I sent the following message to all volcanoes: 'Mark Twain stops animen.' If I do not counter it every day, it will go out to the human realm. Should I become incapacitated or die in the interim, it will be broadcast, and you will lose your animen. That will likely complicate your program, Mr. V."

"You took out an insurance policy."

"What else? It isn't as though we trust each

other."

The man gazed at her. "Damn. I like your style."

"I don't like yours. Now let's adjourn to your sub to negotiate."

He smiled. "This way," the clone said, leading them to the starboard, which was the right side of the yacht when facing forward. There was the sub, nestling close, its top hatch open. "Sorry I can't join you, but it's a private meeting."

They jumped across and climbed single file down the ladder into the sub. The hatch closed, shutting them in. They were in a small modestly illuminated chamber. Subs weren't known for spaciousness or for wasted power.

A svelte young woman appeared. She wore long blond hair, a tight blouse, and a very short skirt. "Hello, Bull and Lavender. I am Templa."

"The telepath!" Lavender exclaimed, surprised. It was right there in the woman's mind. The Bull just looked, as she was an eyeful.

Templa smiled. "You were looking for a male, lava girl. Mistake."

"Mistake," Lavender agreed. She had missed the obvious again, by limiting her focus to one gender. But she could tell that this woman's powers of mind reading and projection were significantly beyond her own. That was another reason Lavender had missed her: she was better at hiding. She was dangerous.

"We are meeting under truce," Templa said. "Agreed?"

Was there a choice? "Agreed," Lavender said,

and The Bull nodded, his eyes locked on the woman's torso. Lavender was annoyed that his interest was so readily invoked, but what could she say? He was male.

"This way." Templa turned, providing The Bull a view of her pert rear, and led them to a larger chamber where two figures waited in comfortable chairs.

The enemy was throwing curves at them, in more than one sense. Both Lavender and The Bull had been unbalanced, albeit for different reasons. There were certainly rough seas ahead.

"Welcome, visitors." He was a big, powerful bear of a man with white hair. Villainous was the merged man and polar bear. The other man was the real President Walton. "Take your seats."

Lavender and The Bull sat. "The president appreciates your coming," Villainous said. "He hopes you will somehow free him and save humanity, but he doubts your ability to do so." Lavender read the truth of that in the president's mind. He was a thoroughly experienced politician, a realist, who understood the odds against him. Knowing himself to be powerless, he was lying low.

Then Templa took the last seat, opposite them, her skirt not even trying to cover her thighs. "Three of us present are not telepathic," she said, meaning the three males. "Therefore I will translate as necessary."

"You're human!" The Bull said, his eyes not quite reaching the level of her face.

Her lips quirked. "You noticed. To answer your questions, yes I am to be spared the holocaust. I am

Villainous's girlfriend. I am also the leading telepath of the vicinity. It is a business and social relationship. But Vil is not the jealous type, should you be minded to join our cause. I happen to like animen." She smiled at The Bull, who shifted uncomfortably.

"Let's get on to business," Lavender snapped. She was aware that if Templa succeeded in distracting The Bull sufficiently, Lavender would be on her own. Villainous might even use him as a lever against her. There were levels and levels.

True. Lavender almost jumped. That was Templa's projected thought.

"First, the tour," Villainous said smoothly.

"Tour?" Lavender asked, surprised again.

"I will show you Utopia. You need to appreciate what we offer."

"You offer disaster."

"Hardly. Unrestrained humanity offers the disaster. It will not govern itself for the sake of reason. It needs to be stopped before the world is completely ruined for the future of life itself."

"He has a point, Lavender," Templa said. "You know it."

And she could read Lavender's mind to verify it. He *did* have a point.

Still, she fought. "Humanity has its flaws, and some are huge," she conceded. "It needs to be corrected, not destroyed."

"Books have been published on the subject," Villainous said. "Movies have been made and shown. Scientists are overwhelmingly aware. Common sense shows that the human course is wrong. Yet the destruction continues. It will soon enough wipe out most other species, and then mankind itself. Man is doomed. My proposal merely takes man out of the picture while something else remains to be saved. It is, by grim analogy, like a lone man getting to end himself before pointless and hideously expensive medical procedures wipe out all his assets and needlessly impoverish his family. He is being sensible; it is the larger society that is mad."

"You know—" The Bull started.

"Grab my ass," Lavender said, hoping to shut him up.

"Or mine," Templa said. "I will let you talk freely, animan."

The Bull remained loyal to Lavender, but Templa's offer was tempting. He wished he could somehow be allowed to grab both.

And Templa knew it, salaciously reading his mind at the same time Lavender was. She did know what interested animen. Villainous was making progress with The Bull by focusing on his weakness.

"She's full human," Lavender murmured. "Your unbridled passion would kill her."

Templa winced, now reading Lavender's mind. What The Bull considered fondling, anyone else would consider mayhem. "True," she said regretfully.

There was a bump. "And we are here," Villainous said grandly.

"Where?" The Bull asked.

"Utopia," the president said. "It is impressive."

"You've seen it?"

"Templa projected it to my mind. It's like a total immersion internet game."

Lavender was becoming increasingly wary of Templa. But something bothered her: so far it seemed as if Lavender herself were the object of their persuasion, rather than The Bull. Did that make sense?

Smart girl.

Yet Lavender was neither fully human nor an aniwoman. She had no 'Mark Twain' flaw. She was just The Bull's hot stone girlfriend, a creature of no significant account. She should be just a minor obstacle to eliminate.

False.

What was she not picking up on? She needed to know soon, lest any argument she try to make be torpedoed by her ignorance. There was more going on here than a silly tour.

True.

Damn that snooping mind! This was like playing a tennis game blindfolded.

True.

"This way," Villainous said. He stood and led the way back to the entry ladder. They ascended one by one. Lavender was last, following Templa. Those legs! At least The Bull was not getting freaked out by that nether perspective.

I may be your friend.

Lavender very much doubted that.

They were in a larger chamber surrounding the hatch. "This is pressure and heat controlled, of course," Villainous said. "Because we are two miles down, and the pressure and heat would otherwise be lethal. It's actually a shell, a bubble in the rock. It will be much larger, in due course. This is really just a model, a sample. But it shows the direction." They walked out the open door.

And paused, stunned. The vista ahead was of a mountain villa with a grassy slope descending to the valley below. White clouds floated in a blue sky, and sunlight reflected off the surface of a valley lake. Petite picturesque cottages formed a village where two small rivers joined. The air was sweet, with a trifling breeze. A lone deer bounded across a field.

"And there are fish in the lake," the president said. "And corn and wheat growing on the farm."

"This isn't underground!" The Bull exclaimed.

"Ah, but it is, my friend," Villainous said. "Observe." He turned back to the house they had just emerged from and tapped the stone wall with a finger. There was a hollow clink.

The Bull tried it. "Plastic!" he said. He walked to the side and tapped the air beside the house. There was another clink. He drew back his fist.

"Uh-uh," the president cautioned. "You don't want to punch a hole in the facade and let the noxious gas in. The whole scene is a model, as he said. Like a winter blizzard ball you can shake and put down. But we don't want to shake this."

"All fake?" The Bull asked, amazed.

"The inner wall of the shell is painted, as is the sky," Villainous said. "The mock sun crosses it by traveling on its track. But inside the bubble, it is as you see. The air is not generated naturally; it is more like air conditioning so as to keep the local environment fresh and wholesome. We have terraformed this much, and animen are laboring to extend it so that more can reside here. The whole job will take time, but we will have time, once the disruptive folk above are gone."

"Animen," The Bull said. "Let me see them."

Lavender kept silent, happy to let him ask the questions.

"Here." Villainous walked to the edge, found a crevice, and pulled open a panel. He ducked through it, disappearing from view. The Bull followed, and then the others. Templa and Lavender were the last, again.

"How can we be friends?" Lavender demanded quietly.

"When we are on the same side." The woman ducked through the aperture, and Lavender followed. She had hoped to provoke a more informative response. So much for that.

There was a short passage leading to another dome, but this one was quite different. It was like a mine, and smelled of sweat and rock dust. Animen and aniwomen were working with sledgehammers to break up rock at the base and sides, enlarging the space. "We don't use power tools here," Villainous explained. "Too difficult to process the pollutive exhaust in this confined space. We do use fossil fuels to power the larger equipment that forms the initial chambers, drawing from the virtually inexhaustible supply in the low layers. That pollution gets piped down below. We do not want to mess up our realm the way the humans are doing in theirs. Utopia has to be climate controlled."

They returned to the first bubble. "This doesn't seem too bad," The Bull said to Lavender. Yes, they were impressing him.

"Remember, it's just a sample, a show," she said. "It could be prettied up, unlike the reality."

"It is," Villainous said. "But it presages the reality. We intend to have the full enclave every bit as nice as this."

There was a false note here. This was not adding up. Lavender had sent out the "Mark Twain" information to protect herself, but now she doubted they cared about that. What was their real concern? "And what *is* the reality?" she demanded. "What do you really want of us?"

"We need your help, Lavender," Templa said. "We may not be able to do it without you. Wiping out the humans will be pointless if we can't make a viable population to replace them."

"What are you talking about? We're your enemies!"

"We need you as our friends."

"This is crazy!"

"No," Villainous said. "This is reality. We really are trying to save the world, but not humanity, which we feel is beyond redemption. But we have one potential opponent who can destroy it all. We need to nullify that opponent at the outset, lest all our efforts be wasted."

"What are you talking about?"

"The volcanoes. We are setting up beneath bedrock, working our way down. Below us is the magma. The volcanoes can raise it at any time and wipe us out. Their minions can read our minds; they know precisely what we're doing. They can strike at any time they choose. We need to be sure they won't. That is why we need a deal with the lava folk."

"I don't believe this!"

"Show her, Templa."

"Read my mind," Templa said, and laid it open.

There it was, spread out like a gourmet banquet. Everything relevant, without restrictions on the irrelevant, in case Lavender wanted to verify the larger picture. It was impossible to deceive, this way. The woman had laid herself out like a virgin on an altar, completely vulnerable to the men of the tribe.

And it was all true. They were building Utopia. They needed a deal with the volcanoes. They were not offering to save mankind.

Again, which side was she on?

Chapter 21:
Death

I scratched my chin, watching Lavender watch Templa.

That the woman I had come to have some strong feelings for—sex and saving the world will do that to a guy—was having a wide range of emotions was obvious. I had no clue what the telepath, Templa, was showing Lavender. Nor was I sure I wanted to.

"She's in conflict, Vil," said Templa, blinking and stepping back.

"Understandable," said the massive polar bear. Come to think of it, maybe I needed a catchy name, too. The Bull was rather obvious. Villainous didn't go around calling himself Polar Bear. He called himself Villainous

"And this one," said Templa, jutting a thumb at me, and surprising me with her ability to read two minds at once, "is busy wondering what name he should choose for himself. Apparently, he's not happy with being called The Bull."

"Simple thoughts," said the massive white bear, "for a simple man."

I considered taking offense to his words, until I realized that, yeah, for the most part, I was simple.

"The simplest of men," said Templa disdainfully.

Truth was, I enjoyed living a simple life. I enjoyed drinking, playing pool, watching football, and working as a rodeo clown—which could be damn exciting at times. I hadn't asked for any of this. But I decided to let it go. Now wasn't the time to let loose, but I sure hoped it came soon. My horns were veritably itching to tear through all this plastic crap.

"Horny wants to destroy something," said Templa.

"A classic bull in a china shop," said Villainous. "Or, in this case, a bull in Utopia."

I lowered my head. A man—or bull—could only take so much.

"Bull, wait!" said Lavender.

"Why?" I asked, and wondered if that was actual steam I could see wafting up from my nostrils. "So that you can have time to decide to join them or not?"

"Is their offer so terrible, Bull? This place has potential. And he's right, we are the freaks up there," she said, pointing vaguely up. How far below we were, I hadn't a clue. She continued, "Down here..."

"Down here, you are with brothers and sisters," finished Villainous.

"That you created," I said.

Villainous, whose tufts of white fur scattered over his broad face made him look almost elderly, smiled and said, "My children."

I shuddered at the thought.

"You know," I said, lowering my head some more. "I never asked for this shit. I never asked to be turned. And yet you did it anyway. You made me into what I am. And you know what? That just pisses me off."

"Oh, how I would love to have a shut-off switch for you, old boy," said Villainous. "Perhaps there is some way to convince you to join our cause?" He snapped his fingers. Like me, part of him was human, and although long, dark claws stretched out from his fingers, his hands were just that: human hands. Big hands, granted, with thick tufts of white fur along the back of them. Just as he snapped his fingers, a panel in a nearby wall opened and three women appeared. All were nude, and all were shivering. The sight of them, however, had the opposite effect, especially when I saw that some sported lash marks.

"Human playthings," said Villainous. "I couldn't, after all, let all of humanity go to waste."

"And on that note," said the president, stepping forward. "Are you no better than the men above, the governments above, the corporation above? Sure, some of their practices might be destroying the world, but there are many good people up there fighting to save it. Your solution is to accelerate the destruction. Which is no solution at all."

The giant polar bear turned his massive head

toward the president. "I don't call myself Villainous for nothing, Mr. President. The nukes, which you will soon authorize to launch—"

"Like hell I will!"

Villainous ignored the president's protest. "Will launch only at the biggest cities in the world. The initial destruction will wipe out more than half of the human population. The rest will be dispatched over time with my special anti-primate remedy."

"Poison," said the president, seething. He was a good man, despite the fact that I had not voted for him.

"Of course. As you can see, I have an affinity towards animals. I do not wish to see the earth completely destroyed, or to harm more animals than is necessary. I only wish to see man, the real plague, removed."

"And who are you to decide the fate of mankind?"

"Who am I indeed? Templa, show them."

His shapely telepath nodded, and what came next was an onslaught of images and memories, all culled from Villainous and broadcast to those of us in the room. Yes, Templa was a powerful telepath indeed.

What I gathered from the barrage of visions and scenes was of a troubled scientist, a genius before his time, who had been badly disfigured growing up. Indeed, this young genius had endured ridicule and pain that few would ever understand. He had first used his great mind to devise a way out of his limited apparatus, and into something very,

very powerful. I next saw series after series of experiments, many of which had gone horribly wrong, and many good men and creatures had to be put down. I had been one of the first successful blends, apparently. And it had been entirely by accident. Wrong place and time. Well, that explained that.

Shortly, he improved upon his experiments, and in the intervening years, had mastered the process, so much so that he had created an army...and had given himself a powerful new body. And, apparently, a desire to end the human race.

"So kids were mean to you," I said, when the visions had ended. "Is that any reason to take out your pain on the entire world? There are many good people on earth. Many people helping other people."

"And if I could save them, I would." And the villain merely shrugged his hulking, muscle-packed shoulders. Yeah, he was certainly no longer the deformed boy in a wheelchair.

"So that's it, then?" said the president. "You had a rough life, and so the rest of the world must suffer?"

"Partly," said Villainous, and now he strode around our little group. Like me, his lower half was all animal. Or mostly animal. He sported a fuzzy little nub of a tail that was almost comical. "I realized that I was put on earth for a reason."

"Really, now?" said the president. The man had, as my dad would say, *chutzpah*. "I am, after all, part of nature too. So, why would the world give birth to someone like you?"

"A psychopath like you?" I asked.

"A genius like me," said Villainous, and he continued to circle our group. I kept my eyes on the furry bastard. "I realized it was to put my great intellect to use."

"To destroy?"

"To rebuild. I am here for a reason, ladies and gentleman, and that reason is to purge the earth."

"Jesus," said the president, turning to me. "Someone has a God complex."

"Lucky for us," said Villainous, "that we need only your retinal scan and fingerprints to unlock the launch sequence." I noticed again that the president was sporting a small briefcase. A briefcase that Villainous snatched from him with one great paw. "My clone, of course, can do the rest."

"What are you saying?" asked the president.

"I'm saying, there is no more need to keep you alive."

With one quick thrust, a set of twelve-inch bloody claws appeared from the president's chest. The man struggled briefly, gasped, and then slumped forward.

The President of the United States was dead.

And that's when I charged.

Chapter 22:
Shunt

Several thoughts tumbled through Lavender's conscious-ness in that instant.

One was that Villainous had deliberately provoked The Bull to violence. He *wanted* a good fight, and to get rid of an animan he could not directly control. Another was that Villainous would not have done it had he not been sure of winning. Fair play was not a significant part of his repertoire, as his slaughter of the president showed. Yet The Bull was if anything stronger physically than the Bear, and he had been fighting folk throughout, while Villainous had been dallying with captive human women while planning his holocaust. He was probably out of shape, physically, despite his passion for violence. So what was his secret weapon?

And there was Templa, watching the fight with interest as The Bull collided with the Bear. She was the weapon! She could project thoughts, which meant she could probably mess with The Bull's mind and render him unable to fight effectively. She didn't need the Mark Twain logic gate. Suppose she turned off his sight, or stunned him so that he was vulnerable to the Bear's attack? How could Lavender protect him from that? Well, maybe there was a way, if she could set it up. A long shot, but if it worked—

She had to act quickly. Using the cover of The Bull's nearly mindless rage, she sent another message to the lava folk for them to relay to the volcano. *Shunt!* Would they understand the accompanying sentiment? Maybe not, but maybe the volcano would. It was after all in touch with other volcanoes, including her grandfather. Grandfather knew how she thought. But it had to be fast, within minutes if feasible. Seconds, if possible.

Templa glanced at her. "What are you up to, lava girl?" she asked. "I had better see."

Before she could follow up with a probe into Lavender's mind, Lavender charged her. She knocked the human woman back against the wall. She was far stronger physically than the telepath, just as The Bull was with respect to the Bear. Templa could not focus mentally at the moment; she had to save her own lovely ass.

Meanwhile the two males were having a blast. The Bull was swinging fists while the Bear was gouging with claws, each scoring repeatedly on the other. The pain of their wounds radiated out, but neither cared. The smell of blood only revved them up further. This was what combat was all about, and they reveled in it.

Stupid males, Lavender thought.

Agreed, Templa responded. *Stop foolishly attacking me like a thoughtless male and see the light. You are destined for great things in the new order. Villainous likes you.* She sent a picture of the Bear kissing her naked flesh. Lavender was revolted. She would never let such a monster get at her body.

Forget it, witch! Lavender took hold of her by the shoulders and shook her. *My doubts were quelled the moment Villainous gratuitously killed the president. My body is not for the likes of that. I'll never join you now.*

Too bad. You'd like the Bear's hug. Now the telepath fought back, using her strength of mind. Suddenly Lavender's vision clouded; it was as if she had blundered into thick fog. But she still had hold of the woman, knowing better than to let her go.

The fog cleared, leaving her standing on a rocky summit. All around her the slope dropped down toward a turbulent sea far below. Wind tore at her, almost pushing her off the pinnacle.

How could this be? She could not have been teleported from the underworld to such a distant site. Templa had a powerful mind, but there had been no sign of such ability when she read it.

Then there came a speck in the sky. A bird flying toward her. A large one. A very large one. In fact, it was a winged dragon.

That was the giveaway. Dragons were popular in fantasy, but they had never actually existed.

Credulous primitives had found the giant bones of dinosaurs and conjectured their fantastic origin. Thus the wild stories of fire-breathing monsters. What reptile had ever breathed fire? It was rubbish. This was an illusion, nothing more.

The dragon oriented on her and blew out a blast of fire that would have toasted any ordinary person who failed to leap off the mountain. That was evidently the design: to trigger an involuntary reaction to avoid getting badly burned. To make the victim plunge into the surrounding sea, where hungry water monsters surely lurked. But Lavender was no ordinary person. If there was one thing she had no fear of, it was fire. She was a creature of the fire, of a volcano. So she stood her ground and took the blast on her chest.

Her clothing puffed into ashes and went up in smoke. Oh, she had been dressed for this, in the vision? Now she was smokily naked but unburned. "Come and get it, big boy," she called to the dragon.

Could this be a fantasy game Templa played with the Bear? He would hug the dragon, whose body would feel like the woman's, and they would make mad love? So it had been adapted to terrorize Lavender. But she simply did not fit the frame. If she got hold of the dragon, she would make short work of it.

If? She had been holding Templa when this scene came on, as she had remembered. She had not let go. She could take control of this vision. She reached out and caught the tail of the dragon as it swooped past her. She hauled it in close. It did feel

145

like a woman. In a moment, she had the telepath in her embrace. Well now.

Templa struggled, but Lavender muscled her into position for a hot kiss. Very hot. There was a stifled scream, and it wasn't her own.

The vision dissolved. "Help!" Templa cried through burnt lips.

Villainous paused in his own bear hug with The Bull. He reached out and caught Lavender by the shoulder. He hurled her against the wall. Templa fell away, sobbing through scorched lips.

The Bull, seeing his opening, leveled a thunderous blow, smashing Villainous in the face. The animan fell to the floor. The Bull dived for him before he could recover his feet, ready to finish the job.

"Do it!" Villainous cried to the woman.

Templa visibly focused on The Bull. She was sending the kill thought!

Villainous collapsed. The Bull stood over him uncertainly. Was he faking?

No. The animan was unconscious or dead.

"What happened?" The Bull asked, bewildered. "I didn't hit him that hard."

"It was the shunt," Lavender said. "The protection against cheating."

"The what?"

"I had the volcano put a mental shunt in your head," she explained. "It didn't do anything itself; it was inert. You didn't feel it at all. But when Templa sent the knockout or kill thought, the shunt bounced it off you and to Villainous. He got blasted. He's a victim of friendly fire."

"Templa tried to kill me?"

"Or cripple you so Villainous could kill you. She was his secret weapon. He had no intention of fighting fair."

"The bastard!"

There was a groan. Templa was sitting on the floor. She was looking at the fallen Bear. "You killed him!" she said through ragged lips.

"No, you did," Lavender told her. "It was your mental blast that felled him. You got the wrong target."

The woman looked at her. Then her tears turned to fury. "Well, I won't get the wrong target again."

Lavender knew that the telepath could strike mentally before either of them could reach her. Templa was probably more dangerous now than Villainous would have been. This battle was not yet over.

Chapter 23:
Impasse

"Be smart, Templa," said Lavender. "You *did* hit the right target. Your blast rebounded and hit Villainous instead. Bull is protected, and so am I. Your mental blast could very well have rebound and hit you."

I knew I was protected, but I hadn't known Lavender was, although it stood to reason. Why not also protect one of their own? Then again, I didn't know much about any of this. I was a simple man, after all. They were right about that. Indeed, I lived to drink and fight and copulate—and not necessarily in that order. Villainous had proven to be a worthy opponent, too. It had been a glorious battle that had ended far too soon. Indeed, one moment I had been locked-up in mortal combat—and loving every second of it—and the next, Villainous was lying on the ground, seemingly dead.

I looked down at the many wounds inflicted by the massive white bear and his razor sharp claws and teeth. Already the wounds were healing. Whatever mad science had created me, had also infused me with rapid cell regeneration. Before my very eyes, my wounds were healing and closing and disappearing altogether. Only the fresh splatters of blood remained.

"Yes, Bull, you were designed to regenerate," said Templa, although I don't think she was reading my mind. Reading my body language was more like it. "You were, in fact, designed to live a long, long time."

"He's immortal?" asked Lavender.

"Not quite, but close. His skin cells are configured to replace themselves immediately..." She knelt down and ran a hand over the bear's bloodied face. I had done a number on him. I noted that he wasn't regenerating. He just lay there, unmoving.

"My *death thought*, as I call it, can effectively shut down a brain," said Templa. "Or, more accurately, fry a brain. He's quite dead. Such a shame. He was a worthy lover and a devoted follower."

"Follower?" asked Lavender.

"Yes, follower. Polar Bear made such a good Villainous, don't you think? Very convincing."

"Then who's Villainous..."

"She is, Bull," said Lavender. "Polar Bear was a fake. He was only pretending. Or being compelled to pretend."

"Maybe a little of both," said Templa, shrugging. "Perhaps you two failed to note Polar Bear's claws? Hard to do serious lab work without opposable thumbs." She studied me. "I am reminded of the old riddle where a father and son are in a car accident. The father dies instantly, and the son is transported to the nearest hospital. Once there, the doctor comes in and exclaims: 'I can't operate on this boy.' 'Why not?' one of the nurses asks. And the doctor responds: 'Because he's my son.'"

"This is hardly a time for riddle—" began Lavender.

"I don't get it," I said, cutting in. "I thought the dad had died."

Lavender elbowed me in the ribs. "The doctor is his mother, you big dope."

"Ah," I said, nodding. "*Now* I get it."

"And that's the problem: the world is full of dopes," said Templa. "Chauvinistic dopes, powerful dopes. Dopes who will do all they can to keep us women down, to subjugate us, torment us, rape us, and give us far less than our fair share. Even a girl who, at the age of fourteen, had been top of her class at MIT. A girl who would go on to be the leading geneticists of her time, a girl who had been forced, time and time again, to prove herself to far inferior males. A girl who had removed herself from society. A girl who had used her family's vast fortune to create everything you see before you. Even you, Bull." She paused, breathing deeply. She had gotten herself worked up. "Of course, much of my plan involves rebuilding *under* the earth while the surface radiation dissipates. To do that, I need to reach an agreement with the lava folk. Their magma chambers would make ideal cities. Not to mention, I do not wish a war with them." She looked at Lavender. "That's where you come in."

"Forget it. No way in hell I'm helping you destroy the world."

"I could try to coerce you. You are, after all, surrounded by a small army of animen."

"Two words," I said. "Mark Twain."

Templa nodded. "Exactly. With those two words, you could effectively render my army into a pack of mindless animals." She looked at Lavender. "Not to mention, if any harm came to you, I suspect this cavern would boil over with magma."

"You can say that again, sister," said Lavender. "So you can tell your human guards to lower their weapons."

"You sense them?" asked Templa, surprised.

"Ten of them, scattered throughout the plastic city."

"Very good, Lava girl. You are stronger than I thought. Maybe even stronger than you thought, too."

"Just remember," said Lavender, "if we die, the lava folk attack."

"Understood," said Templa, bowing slightly. "The human guards are simply my assurance that Bull Boy doesn't gore me to death. I don't have to read minds to know what he's thinking."

I blinked. She was right, of course. I had, indeed, been thinking that most of this problem goes away if Templa suddenly found herself on the wrong end of one of my long horns.

"I die, and we all die," said Templa.

"Understood," said Lavender. "Like you said,

an impasse. What, then?"

Templa took in a lot of air. "I spent years planning for this moment. Down to the last detail. What I hadn't planned on was either of you or the lava folk. What's the old saying... the best-laid plans of mice and men often go awry."

"Very apropos," said Lavender.

Templa, or Villainous, sighed. "And since I have effectively assassinated the President of the United States, I will be on the run for the rest of my life."

"And no doubt planning the future destruction of the earth?" quipped Lavender.

"Oh, that is a given," said Templa, winking.

I could be wrong—and I hoped like hell I was wrong—but these two seemed to be getting along. Hell, it was as if they were bonding or something.

I stepped forward, ready to put a stop to this. "Well, I for one want to get the hell out of here."

"That can be arranged."

"And no funny business," I said.

"I assure you there will be none."

"So says the woman who had no problem murdering billions," I mumbled.

"We all have dreams," said Templa, shrugging. "The world needs a good villain, and I am more than happy to fulfill that role." She cocked her head to one side, as if listening to someone invisible next to her. "Now, if you two are ready, your submersible awaits."

Chapter 24:
Proposal

Lavender did not trust this. Templa was letting them go? How would that resolve the impasse?

She did not need to read a mind to figure that one out. By detonating the sub and destroying them both without a fight. Then Templa would be free to pursue her agenda without opposition. It could be made to look like an accident.

Smart girl.

Except for the automatic revelation of the Mark Twain code if Lavender died. Had Templa forgotten that?

Oops.

Lavender put her mind into interference mode. "Distract her," she told The Bull.

He looked at her, surprised. "Not kill her?"

"Not yet. If you kill her, the lurking humans we can't stop via Mark Twain will spray this chamber with bullets and you'll be dead. I don't want that to happen. You're tough, but not that tough."

"You won't be dead?" he asked.

"I can't be killed with bullets. At least, not here. There's too much hot stone in me. You're the one in danger. So distract her. Kiss her if you have to. Her mind is treacherous, but her body is real, and it's the kind you like. Have some fun with her, but keep her busy."

"What are you up to?" Templa asked. "I can't read your mind now."

"I'm not the telepath you are," Lavender said. "But I can block you out." Then to The Bull: "Do it." Meanwhile, she kept her mind clouded. Templa might read it anyway if she had time to fully focus, but probably not when she had to deal with The Bull at the same time.

He looked dubious, but he trusted her. "Maybe a small kiss."

"I'll fry your brain, cow boy," Templa said derisively.

"Not with the shunt. Go ahead; blast me. You'll only wipe out yourself." He advanced on her.

Templa raised a hand. "One word or one signal from me will get you shot dead, bull turd. They have explosive bullets that will tear you to pieces too small to heal. I am holding off only because I prefer to keep you as leverage against the lava girl."

"And if you take me out, you'll have no leverage at all," he said. "I got that. Then she'll kill you by burning you to death. I'm betting you'd rather make out with me than have to kill me and face her wrath." He caught her raised hand and drew her in to him. "Hey, she's right: your sexy body's real."

"You ignorant oaf! You think you can take my lover's place?"

"Yeah, since you didn't really care for him either." He bore her back against the wall. "You said you liked animen, remember? You showed me your shapely butt. Okay, let me at it." He grabbed her butt.

"You insufferable beast!" She struck at him with her free hand.

"Praise will get you nowhere," he said, not even trying to dodge the blow. She couldn't hurt him physically.

He was doing a nice job. Lavender had her mind on interference, and could not read Templa any more than the woman could read her, but knew she was outraged. It wasn't that Templa had any objection to making out with a man, any man or animan; it was that she wanted it to be on her terms, not his. Feminist that she was, she hated the notion that he could feel her up with impunity, as if she were just a passing prostitute. Lavender appreciated that aspect; she felt much the same. Her relationship with The Bull was by her choice; any other man would get burned, literally. Which was why this was such a good distraction: Templa was letting her emotions interfere with her sensible curiosity about what was on Lavender's mind.

Lavender put her body on auto-pilot, doing what she had laid out for it. Meanwhile, she reviewed the mental situation. Templa's "Oops" rang false. She had not forgotten the Mark Twain caution. So why was she ready to kill Lavender and set it loose?

The same reason Villainous had killed the president: they no longer needed him alive. For a few hours, his fingerprints and retinas would remain sharp; they could carefully cut off his fingers and pull out his eyeballs and use them.

And that gave her the clue. Templa had now read Lavender's mind thoroughly enough to be able to emulate it in thought. That might even be the reason for their physical meeting. She could send the 'postpone' signal, and the volcano would not know the difference. She no longer needed Lavender alive. She could kill Lavender by isolating her from the ground and blowing her up in the sub. She wasn't letting them go at all; she was tricking them into their doom.

"You unutterable turd!" Templa exclaimed. "Get your bovine muzzle off my breast!"

The Bull did not answer. It seemed that his mouth was busy. Lavender had shown him the way of that. He was after all enjoying his chore.

"Huh?" But that was him now. What had happened?

"You thought the kill signal was the only one in my arsenal?" Templa demanded. "How do you like making out with a crocodile?"

Oh no! She had made her body resemble that of the reptile, at least in appearance and sensation. Crocodiles lacked human lips, buttocks, or breasts, and a reptile belly just wouldn't taste the same. No wonder he was out of sorts. Lavender had to admire her versatility.

"Or a dragon?" Lavender knew how the woman

could conjure a seeming dragon. She was turning the tables on The Bull without actually hurting him. "How do you think I controlled the bear man, you idiot? I could be anything he wanted—or didn't want, depending on my mood."

But he had done his job. Templa had been distracted long enough. "It's okay, Bull," Lavender called. "You can let her be now."

The Bull backed away from the scaly creature. "I know it's an illusion, but it's a mean scaly illusion," he said, disgruntled.

"What was the point of all that?" Templa demanded, reappearing in a somewhat mussed state. "We're still at an impasse, and might as well separate."

"We're still at an impasse," Lavender agreed. "But the situation has changed. Look at the president."

"He's dead, but we can still use his prints and —" Templa broke off. "Oh, no!"

"What the hell happened to him?" The Bull asked. "His hands are gone, and his eyes are smoldering."

"I burned out his fingers and eyes," Lavender said. "While you distracted Miss Crocodile and I kept my mind masked. Now those prints can't be used to validate deployment of the American nukes."

"But that means—"

"No more nuclear threat," Lavender finished smugly.

"You bitch!" Templa exclaimed. "You set him on me while you did your dirty work."

"You thought reading minds was the only thing in my arsenal?" Lavender inquired sweetly. "You're free to kill us now, but we're also free to kill you. Since it's not safe for us to use the sub, we might as well stay here and finish you off, The Bull in his way, and I in mine, should your minions try to interfere. That should be interesting."

Templa was clearly a tough minded realist. "We have nulled each other, for the moment," she agreed. "What is on your mind, volcano spawn?"

"I thought you'd never ask, crocodile snot. I believe it is time for us to compromise."

The woman considered. "It seems I underestimated you. I assumed you were just another crossbreed variant like the animen. What kind of compromise do you propose?"

"We don't actually have to fight, or face mutual destruction. What you're doing below ground is worthwhile. Curbing the human decimation of the topside planet is also worthwhile. If we work together we just might improve things."

"I doubt we can work together," Templa said grimly.

"There may be a way. We have solid reasons to distrust each other. But I think it has been established that the animen are really no better than the humans, and I'm not even sure that the lava folk are perfect either. Destroying any one type will merely allow the others to prevail, prosper, and become corrupted by their dominance, to the detriment of the planet. We can't trust any of them with ultimate power. Maybe if we combine our resources we can facilitate the colonization of other planets, where humans can settle alone, or animen, or lava folk. We are going to need new worlds; Earth is almost exhausted at this point. There's no point in wiping out mankind along with most of the other creatures, when left unchecked mankind will soon enough do that for himself. Destruction will not usher in the braver new world."

"I disagree. But assuming you are correct, what can we do?"

"We can install new leadership that will labor to turn the corner and put mankind, animankind, and lavakind on a course to global sustainability, whether on Earth or other planets. To truly cut pollution, global warming, overpopulation, depletion of diminishing resources. It may take centuries to see the result, but it's the direction that counts."

"And who exactly can be trusted to provide such leadership?"

"You, me, and The Bull, to start. We do have our special talents."

Templa laughed. "It's an illusion to think we're not corruptible."

"After we prepare a governing template of the ideal qualities of perfect leadership. And submit ourselves to be the first recipients of that template. Which will be installed by the telepathic power of the volcanoes, who really don't care what happens to life on Earth as long as it leaves them alone. They are, in this respect, objective."

Templa stared at her. "You're serious!"

Lavender smiled somewhat grimly. "The template would include our mutual desires to support and trust each other, and to be worthy of that trust, and to work unstintingly for the common good. And to recruit other telepaths and skilled individuals to join the cause. It would cost us our ornery freedom of choice but make us reliable."

Templa shook her head. "I have to think about this."

"Don't we all! Salvation does not come cheap."

Chapter 25:
Escape

While Templa mulled the offer over, we waited in a structure that resembled a grand ballroom. The air was clean and fresh. The plastic structure served to keep the noxious gas at bay. I suspected the gas wouldn't have much effect on Lavender, but I sure as hell didn't want to breathe it.

Just prior to dropping us off, Templa had said that the plastic city was made of material of her own creation. She wasn't a mad scientist for nothing. Additionally, a fleet of orca men, whale men, and dolphin men, had steadily brought supplies and building material down into this vast underground chamber—a chamber that had been hollowed out eons before by folk history had yet to record. Templa conjectured that this, in fact, might be the remnants of Atlantis—or another long lost kingdom —now swallowed up by the sea. Perhaps from the volcano now simmering below. Meanwhile, a team of animen builders had constructed the city, as they were doing even now, pushing deeper and deeper into the earth, following long-carved out caverns and natural lava tubes. I suspected Lavender would be at home here.

Finally, I eased down on a very real wooden chair. I always eased down on wooden chairs. Trust me, I've broken my fair share of chairs over the intervening bullish years. The room was a storage room of sorts, filled with all manner of wood and metal panels, furniture, and machinery. Apparently not everything was plastic. One thing was obvious: Villainous, or Templa, had thought of everything.

"Exactly," thought Lavender, and I could tell she was running some interference between us and Templa, who was undoubtedly somewhere nearby. "She put a lot of thought and effort and time into this plan."

"She's not going to give it up easily," I thought, nodding.

"She's the queen bee here. The animen and women are her worker bees. Why give this up for altruistic reasons? She doesn't have an altruistic bone in her body. She's drunk on power and revenge. I'm afraid nothing will stop her."

"Maybe you're wrong. Maybe she really is considering your proposal."

"There's one way to know..."

And Lavender got that far-off look in her eye that she gets when she's going deep within. I don't go deep within. Hell, I've never gone deep within. The deepest I got was trying to decide if I was too drunk for another beer.

A moment later, Lavender blinked. She was back. "The lava folk have confirmed my fears."

"How so?"

"They couldn't read her mind—she's even too powerful for them—but they could read the minds of her surrounding minions. They are planning to attack us here, in this room; in fact, within a matter of minutes."

"But if they attack us, won't the lava folk retaliate, and burn these caverns?"

"She's apparently aware of that, and had made plans with her submersible captain to escape, along with the presidential clone."

"The clone," I said, snapping my fingers.

Lavender nodded. "Apparently, there's a Plan C to her attempt to take over the world."

"Rule via the fake president."

"A president she has complete control over," said Lavender.

"We can't let her escape."

"I agree," said Lavender, "which is why I've already summoned the lava folk."

"They're coming now?" I asked, sitting forward.

"Oh, yes. A whole army of them."

Gunfire suddenly erupted, followed by a loud, blaring alarm. Bullets crisscrossed through the air, puncturing through the plastic walls. Many just missing us.

"Let me guess," I said, ducking. "They're here."

"Good guess," said Lavender.

***

My hide was tough enough to withstand most ordinary bullets. Only a direct hit to the head, or one of those explosive bullets would probably kill me. Then again, my regenerating abilities were off the charts. Who knows. Maybe I would regenerate before I could actually die. I didn't want to find out.

Which is why I grabbed an unfinished metal door with one hand, and Lavender's hand with my other, and charged forward, near the rear of the plastic structure. Mercifully, the bullets were coming from one direction—from the main chamber. Two or three errant projectiles slammed into the door, dimpling it from the inside. One of which was just inches from my head. Yeah, that woulda hurt.

"What's the plan?" asked Lavender when we reached the back entrance.

"Find Templa and stop her."

"That's all you got?" asked Lavender.

"I'm known for my brawn not my brain—let's go!"

I kicked down the door, which was easy enough to do, and we found ourselves in a narrow back alley. A plastic back alley. Screams filled the air, followed by more gunfire, and now a small explosion. The ground shook, which was the last thing I wanted to feel while deep beneath the ocean floor. At least, that's where I think we were. The strong chemical acrid smell was the plastic melting. We needed to get out of here anyway, and fast. I didn't believe much of what Templa said, but I had no reason to doubt that the plastic city kept the poisonous fumes at bay.

"This way," I said, and continued down the alley, to where I was certain the submersible was berthed.

Chapter 26:
Gate Rape

Lavender knew they were in a desperate situation.

They had to avoid the battle while making their way to the sub, and they had to get there before Templa did. But they could not take it alone; Templa would trigger its bomb and they would be blown up. If Templa got on it alone, she would go to the yacht and take over the president clone, and go on from there. So they had to get on it *with* Templa. That of course was serious mischief, because though Lavender could take Templa physically, she could not do so mentally.

Yet there was one possible saving grace. Lavender had tried to convert Templa, because the woman had phenomenal telepathic and intellectual talent and could do enormous good, were she only on the right side. Similarly, Templa wanted to convert Lavender, because she represented immediate access to the lava folk that Templa needed to protect the undersea paradise. They needed each other. They did not have to like each other, but both would be better off on the same side, whichever side that was. They needed to hammer out a compromise.

But how could Lavender win Templa to her side? Any mental engagement was likely to go the other way. Unless—

"Bull," she said. "Take me by the hand and lead me to the sub. Or carry me if you have to. Just get me there. I'm about to tune out."

"You're a terror when you tune out," he said.

"More: don't let Templa board the sub alone. But don't board it without her. We three have to be on it together."

"But—"

"If she gets on it alone, she'll go to the 'yot' and take over the clone and start organizing to take over the human world. With her powers of telepathy and projection she just might be able to succeed. We can't afford to risk that."

"Got that," he agreed. "But—"

"If we get on it without her, she'll use her mind to detonate the bomb on it, and we'll be smithereens. We don't want to risk that either."

"Yeah, we don't," he agreed.

"So we have to be together."

"But can't she mess up your mind?"

"Yes. I can't match her mental ability."

"So being on the sub with her is no good either."

"So it would seem. But we have to do it. It's

our only chance."

"But—"

"Trust me. And cover me with your lecherous thoughts. You'd be making love to me now if it wasn't for the battle. If we survive this, they'll come true." Before he could protest further, she tuned out.

What could he do? She felt him leading her by the hand while his thoughts caressed her body. If there was one thing he could do well, it was imagining sex. It was hard for any other mind to touch hers while that firewall of lust and aspiration surged around her. She had to hunker down mentally herself so as not to get swept up in the storm and wrap her body around his. Templa would find it treacherous going.

Now she tunneled out, mentally, on a tight beam that contacted the lava folk. *Need help. Now.*

They answered her. *We can mark you for extraction from the scene. Our folk won't hurt you.*

No. I need another shunt.

A second one in The Bull?

No. In me.

There was a fractional pause as they assimilated this. *What kind?*

Lavender gave a quick but detailed mental description. It needed to be in one place in her mental scheme, but to appear to be in another. The real shunt needed to seem to be her center of voluntary control.

There was an internal wrench that left her dizzy. *It is done.* They did not need to inquire why she needed it; they had picked that up from her mind.

Lavender came out of it. They were at the sub, waiting on Templa. She kept her thoughts stifled, as if she had been drugged. The woman appeared, hurrying toward it. She saw them. Lavender retreated mentally, clothing herself with a feeling of weakness and frustration. She saw no way to prevail.

"What's with the lava girl?" Templa called.

"She tuned out," The Bull explained. "I think she hit her head or something. I had to drag her here. It's not safe to make out with her in the middle of a battle."

"Well, get out of the way, bully boy. I'm taking the sub. You can stay here and screw her to pieces exactly the way your mind suggests."

"No," he said. "We're taking the sub too. I know that's what she wants."

She hesitated, her mind flicking through Lavender's defeated mind, and The Bull's ongoing lust, then came to a decision. "Very well. You operate the sub while I deal with her. The controls are simple; I'll show you how. I promise you'll get to screw her, and maybe me too, after I'm through with her. She'll do anything you want."

"Great!" He picked Lavender up and carried her into the sub, following Templa.

Could the woman actually believe that The Bull cared for Lavender no more than this? As a tough body to satisfy his physical urges? Or was it that Templa was so sure of her power that she didn't care?

He put her down on a metal bench, then went

with Templa to study the sub's controls. So far so good. Lavender lay there like a slowly recovering victim.

Then the sub was in motion. The Bull was operating the controls, and Templa was back. She did not try to talk to Lavender. She simply laid a hand on her head and plunged into her dazed mind.

It was like a nest of ants swarming over a freshly killed carcass, or maybe one that wasn't quite dead yet. They delved into every aspect, seeking its treasures.

Lavender stirred herself. "What?"

"Be at ease, stone person," Templa said. "I need your help in connecting to the lava folk. Since it seems you won't give it voluntarily, I'm overriding your voluntary control."

"But that's rape!" Lavender protested fuzzily. "Rape of the mind. Of my free will."

"What's a little rape to a creature like you? Almost got it. There." She thrust with a thought that felt like a sword being driven into Lavender's head.

And fell back, literally. "Oh!"

"It was a trap, a roadside bomb as it were," Lavender said. "Another shunt. Only this one led to your own mind. You just knocked out your own free will."

"I—I can undo it," Templa said dizzily.

"First, listen. There is something you need to know. This was not simply a bounce. It was the installation of a logic gate like the one you put in the animen. When it is activated, it will wipe out your mind in a similar manner. But the activation key is not words. It's an intention: the mental effort to corrupt or eliminate it. So you will be committing suicide."

"Suicide," Templa echoed, stunned mentally rather than physically. She knew herself to be a fool to fall into this trap. She had been too eager to wrap it up, and became careless. Exactly as Lavender had hoped.

"Meanwhile, you have a choice," Lavender continued inexorably. "You can either try to avoid or fight it, knowing that you are flirting with your own destruction. Or you can accept that the battle has been fought and you have lost. You can work with me, using your considerable talents to build the animan paradise below the sea, and to find positive ways to turn the tide on mankind's destructive impulses so that the world can be saved rather than destroyed. You can have a good life, with considerable power. Only your design to exterminate most of the human species will be changed."

Templa stared at her. "Damn you!"

Then she fell to the floor. Lavender knew from her mind that she was dead. She had suicided rather than surrender.

"Damn," Lavender echoed.

Chapter 27:
Roommates

Turned out, I was a natural at driving a submersible.

I'd always been a quick study and, really, the thing drove itself once it got moving. Now, as we glided up through the dark water, toward a surface still hundreds of feet above, I finally let myself relax.

With Templa, aka Villainous, lying dead at our feet, Lavender and I had been faced with some tough decisions. And not just for ourselves, but for the entire world. What to do with the body of the real President of the United States?

He had been a brave man, courageous in the face of an unpredictable enemy. He had died a painful death while standing up to said enemy. He deserved better than just to rot here in this forgotten cavern. And so, after deliberating, we had reached an agreement, and I had gone back to fetch the body of the fallen president. In doing so, I had seen first-hand the wrath of the volcano people. The plastic city was in ruins: most of it burning or reduced to plastic slush. The animen and aniwomen hadn't fared much better. I saw their torched, genetically manipulated bones poking up through the melted plastic. Many were frozen in time, in the throes of battle. I felt little sympathy. The animen had chosen sides. Even with the threat of the cut-off switch, they had chosen to follow a woman hell bent on destruction. A decision based on violence rarely ended well for anyone.

The president, who had died away from the plastic city entrance, and thus away from the burning carnage, had been left unscathed. I had scooped him up and returned him to the submersible, stepping over the dead body of the beautiful—but deranged—form of Templa. We had set off immediately after.

I sat back in the seat and, careful of my wide set of horns, laced my fingers behind my head. "There are some who might want to misuse the presidential clone for their own advantage. He's a simpleton, remember. Any telepath could influence him."

"I've considered that," said Lavender. "Which is why he should come back with us."

"With us?"

She nodded. "I've scanned the ship above. There are a handful of mindless animen and aniwomen roaming the deck. However, four secret service agents are still alive, presently locked in the brig, deposited there by the animen before we uttered the cut-off switch. The clone is in the galley, eating nachos without the chips."

"So, he's just eating the cheese?"

"Yes."

My stomach growled. I patted it. "Sounds delicious."

"*Any*way," said Lavender, shaking her head. "Once on the surface, we'll swap the dead president with the living clone. I'll implant the secret service agents with a new memory, one in which the president died fighting for his country, which isn't very far from the truth. He took awful injuries to his body, eyes, and fingers, but never yielded. I'll also wipe their memory clean of ever having seen us."

"Holy smokes, you can do all of that?"

"I didn't know I could, until I saw Templa utilize the full extent of her power. I'm not as strong as her, but I can get close."

"So, no one will know of the underground city."

"No one except the lava folk, who won't care."

I nodded, thinking about it. "And what do we do with the clone?"

Lavender smiled, and steam literally rose from the corners of her lips. "He's going home with you, Bull."

"Say again."

"Meet your new roommate; unless, of course, you want to just toss him overboard."

"I'm not a murderer," I said.

"Neither am I," said Lavender. "Which is why he's going home with you, where you can keep an eye on him."

"Great," I said, although I had a brief and satisfying flash of the clone fetching me beer whenever I needed it.

"Your getting drunk days are over, Bull. Anyway, from what Templa implied, the clone might have a very short life span. He might only be functioning for another few years."

"Lucky me," I said, and crossed my arms over my massive chest.

"We are doing the right thing, Bull," said Lavender. "Neither of us are very political. I suppose I could have controlled him, but such a massive undertaking would be exhausting. No, there is a better man suited for the job, and he is the vice president, a man hand-picked by him," said Lavender, jutting a finger at the presidential corpse I had laid across a bench behind us.

"And there is the matter of the president's relatives," I said.

She nodded. "Ultimately, our little ruse would have been discovered, and they call that treason, if I am correct. Besides, his family deserves to know he died a hero's death, protecting his country and the world. The nation deserves to mourn."

I thought about all this and more as the submersible continued silently up to the surface. I knew the world was filled with more animen and aniwomen. How many had sided with Villainous? All of them? Or just the handful we had seen? How many were there... and could they reproduce? Could *I* reproduce?

"Now, this is a line of thinking I'm enjoying," said Lavender, coming over to my seat and sitting on my lap.

I wrapped my arm around her tiny waist. Her horns were back, jutting up through her hair. I admired her solidarity. It felt like we were a real team.

"A super team," said Lavender.

"Lava Girl and Bull Boy," I said.

"It does have a certain ring to it," she said, and leaned down and kissed me, her own lips searing mine, but I didn't care. My lips were regenerating even as we kissed harder and harder.

To my regret, she pulled away. "Oh, by the way, you will be getting *two* new roommates." She winked.

I grinned and pulled her back toward me. "I'm going to need a bigger apartment."

I might have whimpered as she kissed me harder and deeper than ever before...

The End

About the Authors:

Piers Anthony is one of the world's most prolific and popular authors. His fantasy Xanth novels have been read and loved by millions of readers around the world, and have been on the New York Times Best Seller list twenty-one times. Although Piers is mostly known for fantasy and science fiction, he has written several novels in other genres as well, including historical fiction, martial arts, and horror. Piers lives with his wife in a secluded woods hidden deep in Central Florida.

Please visit him at www.hipiers.com for a complete list of his fiction and non-fiction and to read his monthly newsletter.

J.R. Rain is an ex-private investigator who now writes full-time. He lives in a small house on a small island with his small dog, Sadie, who has more energy than Robin Williams. Please visit him at www.jrrain.com.